cocktails & crushes

katrina marie

For those suffering from burnout, or just the weight of the world right now, I see you. Keep doing you, and take care of yourself!

prologue

THIS IS IT. The last time I'll see my uncle. My chance to say goodbye before he leaves this world. He's had a terrible time of battling cancer, and I'm not ready for him to go yet. If I go in that room, there's no way I'm going to be able to keep it together. Not for him, or anyone else. My face always gives away what I'm thinking without me having to say a word.

All Uncle Max will see is anguish. But I'll do my best to tuck it away. To hide it from his knowing eyes. Deep breath in...and out. Placing my hand on the door knob to his room, I turn it, and hope like hell this won't destroy what's left of me.

There are machines beeping and wires connected all over his body. It wasn't this bad a few weeks ago. He was still able to move around. You'd never know he was sick. Now, he can't even get out of his bed on his own without help.

I don't think I can do this. I can't see him like this. He's frail and thin. What am I going to do without my best friend? Without the person who has championed my ideas since I was a child, sitting on the counter of his bar, stacking cups and refilling bowls with nuts?

My body is already turning around. Ready to flee from this room of sickness, death, and sadness. "Angie," his voice is barely a whisper. It's enough, though. Enough to stop me in my tracks and close the door. There's nothing I wouldn't do for this man, and if that means seeing him now, even though it hurts me far more than it does him, I'll do it.

"Hey, Uncle Max." My steps are slow and careful as I make my way toward his bed. He is set up in the guest room of my parents' house. Once he's gone, I don't know that I'll ever want to come in here again. This was the room we built forts in when Mom and Dad were working late. It became a castle, a cave, and whatever my imagination willed it to be. Now, though, it'll be the room I last saw him in. "How are you feeling?"

"Like I could use a drink," he laughs. It's brittle and weak. My heart sinks even further. "You didn't happen to smuggle some whiskey in here for me, did you?"

Forcing a smile, I shake my head. "I'm pretty sure the doctors wouldn't appreciate that, and it's likely the last thing you actually need."

"Or," he points his finger at me. "It could be exactly what I need. It's not like I can do much more damage, anyway," he sighs and looks up at the ceiling, "I'm practically knocking on the pearly gates, waiting for them to allow me entrance."

How can he joke about death when he's so close? "That's not funny, Max."

"It's true." He holds his hand up, and I place mine in his. "I lived a hard life and made horrible choices, but I'm at peace with that. I need you to be at peace with it, too."

"I don't know if I can be." A tear slips down my cheek,

and I hurry to wipe it away. I need to be strong. For him and myself. "How am I supposed to go for great big things when you're gone?"

He squeezes my hand and pulls me closer to him. "Easy," he whispers, "you do great big things. I'll be watching you along the way." Using what I can only imagine is all of his strength, he lifts his free hand to my face and wipes away my tears. "Which brings me to my next point."

"Which is?" I've given up on trying to hide my fears, sadness, and anger. Anger at the world for taking him from us before we are ready. He's here now, I know that. But knowing he could slip away to that endless sleep at any moment has my nerves buzzing.

"I'm giving you the bar." He waits for my reaction, but I don't give him anything except a blank stare. "Did you hear me? My legacy will now be yours."

"I can't take it." I'm shaking my head. It's too big. Too much. I'm only twenty-five. Hell, I don't even have a career. I've been bartending at his bar to pay rent and get by until I figure out what I want to be when I grow up. My degree in business is okay, but it isn't something I can do much with unless I get more schooling. I barely made it through the bachelor's program. Continuing my education sounds like my own personal hellscape.

"You can and you will." He takes a deep breath. Well, as deep as he can take. It sounds like something is rattling in his lungs and it kills me to hear it. "You are the only person who loves that place as much as me. And, you're the only one I trust with it. That I can trust to make it something more than what it is now."

"I don't know the first thing about running a business." My degree says otherwise, but I need guidance. I need my mentor there to hold my hand and show me the way. To let me know that I'm making the right decisions. "George seems to be doing a good job. Why don't you leave it to him?"

"He's not family, Angie." My uncle's voice is deeper, and lower. It's the same tone he'd have when he was disappointed in whatever rebellious shenanigans I would get into in high school. I never thought I'd hear it again as an adult. I feel like that teenager all over again. He's the only one who could get through to me when my parents couldn't.

"There's always my brother." I will do anything in my power to pass off this responsibility to someone else. Someone who wouldn't turn this place I love into a steaming pile of shit.

"No offense, but your brother doesn't know the ins and outs of the bar. He's good at what he does. He's a rancher, nothing else." This time he's shaking his head. "Why are you fighting me so hard on this? I thought you would be excited."

"Because Uncle Max, I can't do this. Everything I touch goes badly. Friendships, relationships. Everything. I can't let that happen to the bar. The thing you love more than anything."

"You're wrong." That shocks me. "My family is what I love more than anything. My brother, sister-in-law, nephew, and niece." He nods toward me. "Besides, the bar isn't in that great of shape to begin with. You could only go up from here."

"What do you mean it's not in great shape?"

"I made some poor decisions with money. The books aren't in the hole, but it's barely turning a profit." My hand gets another squeeze. "That's where you come in. The place needs someone young, and young at heart, to liven the place up. It needs imagination."

He's crazy if he thinks I'm the person for that. My imagination died when I left childhood to enter the shit-show of adulthood. The fact that he'll be leaving this world before he should be shows how shitty it is. How unfair life can be. "I don't think I'm cut out for that. I'm barely a decent bartender."

"You, my darling niece, are a damn good bartender."

"Then why do half of your customers hate me?" No matter what I do, I can't seem to win them over.

"Because you don't take their shit." He laughs, and this one doesn't sound so bad. Maybe the doctors were wrong. Maybe he has a lot of life to live on this planet. "Most of the people who come in are rough around the edges." I can't help the snort that comes out. "Anyway, they don't like being put in their place by someone half their age and size. For them, it's insulting."

"And you think if I take over, they are just going to roll over and be okay with it?" There's no way in hell. A lot of the bikers that come are as sweet as can be, but some of them are...not so nice. I've had to insert myself between a couple of heated arguments before fists were thrown. Was it dangerous? Absolutely. Did I back down? Not a chance in hell. I've learned a thing or two about stepping into sketchy situations after helping my brother at the ranch. Two full-grown men have nothing on a cow running at you in full force.

"When you take over," he corrects me. "I've already amended my will. It's going to happen regardless of what you think you want." He pauses to see if I will say anything.

I don't. It's not like there's anything I can say. He's already made up his mind, and made it legally binding.

Stubborn man. Mom and Dad wonder where I get it from. They need to look no further than my uncle.

"You can sell it if that's what you choose to do. It'll be your bar once I'm gone." He covers his mouth and coughs. The wet sound is back and I hate it. "But I hope you make this old man proud and turn it into something great."

Fucking guilt trips. I hate them, and he just laid a huge one at my feet. How the hell am I supposed to say no to that? Say no to a man on his literal death bed? That would make me the biggest asshole in the universe, and I will not let him down like that. Not when he had a hand in raising me. "Fine," I pout. "I'll take the bar. But I'm warning you now, I don't know that I'll be able to do anything better than you have."

"You will," his smile is big. My heart squeezes, knowing I can bring him this small bit of happiness. Even if I have my own reservations about it. "I think I want to take a nap, now. Arguing with you takes energy."

A grin crosses my lips and I roll my eyes. The first moment of normalcy since I've entered this room. "Get some rest, Max." I stand, bend over, and kiss his forehead. "I'll come argue with you more in the morning."

"You do that." His eyes drift clothes and his breathing levels out.

* * *

My phone rings, pulling me out of a fitful sleep. The bar is burning and I'm stuck inside with no way out. I glance at the time before answering. It's six thirty in the morning. Who calls at this hour?

"Angie?" Dad's voice cracks on the other side of the

phone. I don't need him to say anything else. My worst fear has happened. "He's gone."

I don't bother responding, I lay the phone down next to me and sob. My dad is still on the line. I'm not sure how much time passes, but I feel my mom's arms wrap around me. I've never been more grateful than I am now to live close to my parents.

The days ahead are going to be horrible, but I'm going to do everything I can to fulfill my promise to Uncle Max.

1

angie

I SWEAR, sometimes adults are as messy as toddlers when they eat. There's almost as much food on the floor around some tables as there was on the plate when we delivered the food. Bussing tables isn't really what I should be doing today, but we're short staffed, as usual, and Tucker, the guy that usually takes care of this, is on his break. If there's one thing I'll always do, it's make sure my employees take their breaks, even if I can't. Keeping employees happy is what will keep them coming to work.

Well, for the most part. I don't know what's going on with so many people calling out all of a sudden. We were over staffed at one point, but now that I need more bodies, I can't find anyone. At least, not anyone with the requirements to work the bar.

Now that the table is clean, I can let Lisa know to seat the next guests. She may be young, but she's damn good at her job. I'm keeping my fingers crossed she'll stick around for the long haul. Customers really mesh well with her. It must be her innocent, baby face.

The neon sign above the bar catches my eye on the way to the host stand. It's taken almost a decade, but I've really made something of this bar. I think Uncle Max would be proud of the progress I've made. There are still a few things that need finetuning, but at least I'm not getting payment demands from the bank anymore. When I was finally able to pay off the rest of the mortgage on this place, I breathed a sigh of relief. Everything from here on out is straight profit. Not a bad place to be after all the years my uncle and I have put into this place. Nothing can kill my good mood.

Lisa is adding a name to the wait list when I approach the stand, and I let her finish. "Table six is ready for whoever is next."

"Thanks," she grins, bouncing up and down on her toes. She's so bubbly, and I try to think if there was ever a time in my life where I was the same way. Nope, can't think of one.

"No problem," I knock on the wooden stand with my knuckles. "Let me know if you need anything."

I turn to head back to the bar, but she touches my elbow, lightly. "Actually, there's someone waiting for you outside."

There weren't any meetings noted on my calendar. "Who?"

Her wince tells me all I need to know. "A guy. He said Stella set up a blind date with you. What do you want me to do?"

As much as I love Stella, I'm going to murder her. After her and Johnny became serious, she quickly became one of my best friends. But she has it in her head that if she can find happiness with someone, then she can find someone for me to share my happiness with. For the record, I'm totally okay with being single. I go out and have fun, of course. I've just never found someone that piques my interest.

I could have her lie and say I'm busy. Or, I could literally slip out the back door. No, neither of those options work. Lisa deserves better than having to cover for me. "Tell him to meet me at the bar. Down by the end so I can jump in and help if I need to."

Fingers crossed they'll need me. The nights here are insane, but lunch is still pretty busy. We have some of the best wings in town and everyone comes here for their lunch meetings, or to get away from the office.

"Are you sure?" She glances toward the door. "I can always tell him to come back another day."

"Yeah, I'm sure." Though, I'm grateful she'd do that for me. "Might as well get it over with. If not, I'll have Stella on my ass."

"Good point," she nods. "She's like a dog with a bone when it comes to fixing people up."

"I take it she's on your case, too?"

"Yep." She grabs a couple of menus. "I don't want to settle down, yet. There's so much I want to do on my own. Anyway, I'll show the folks to table six then I'll direct your date to the bar."

"Thanks." As much as I don't want to see this random guy, I should probably make a quick stop in the bathroom and make sure I'm presentable. I don't want to be waiting on him and seem eager. Especially since I never agreed to this in the first place.

* * *

Please, someone have an emergency. Need more of something. Ryan? Roger? Hell, I don't even remember what his name is, but the amount of information he's spewing about stocks and financial math is seconds away from putting me into a hundred-year sleep. You know, maybe like Snow White. Except instead of a poison apple, it's math that does me in. Then let's face it, I'll be sleeping forever. Prince Charming doesn't exist, and I don't particularly want to be saved by anyone. I've worked my ass off to build this bar into what it is today from the dilapidated building it was when Uncle Max had it. With help from Stella, of course.

He must finally notice how much I'm not paying attention because he pauses. "Sorry, I'm boring you, aren't I?"

Shit, do I do the nice thing and say no? Or, say yes? "Not at all," I smile. Though it must come off as more of a sneer because he raises his eyebrows. "Math just isn't really my thing. Unless, you're talking about the ratios of mixed drinks, it pretty much goes over my head." There. A combination of both. I'm not lying, either. I've never been a math person. Even with all my business classes, I barely passed the ones that were strictly math based.

He nods in understanding. "I get it. Sometimes I forget there are people in the world that don't love math as much as I do." He glances at the shelves of liquor behind the bar. "How did you come to own the bar?"

Of course, that would be what he's leading with since I'm giving off the I hate numbers vibe. "My uncle left it to me when he passed away. It was kind of his dying wish that I turn this bar into something amazing." Yep, perfect way to kill the mood.

"Oh, I'm sorry. I-I didn't realize," he stammers over his words.

"It's okay." I pat his arm, reassuring him. "It was a long time ago." I stare at the bottles in front of me and smile. "This was his baby, and after years I've turned it into this. When Stella came here, she saw the potential and helped me bring it to life."

He's slowly nodding. "She's pretty good at that. Whenever she sees a project, she takes it on full force."

"You're telling me." Like this date. To Stella we are both projects. Something she needs to take control of and fix. It's one of the things I love and loathe about her. One day she won't look at me as something broken. She'll see that I'm perfectly capable of handling things on my own. I did it before she showed up in Asheville and I'll keep on. There's no other choice for me. I refuse to ever let this bar fail because of me.

"Do you have any other plans for the bar?" His eyes rove around the room. "Maybe opening up more locations?"

That feels like a loaded question. He's in investment based on his talk of stocks and numbers. While I think that would be amazing, it's not at a point where I'm ready for people to put their own spin in other cities. It's still my baby. "I'm open to more plans, but I don't think I want to franchise." He's opening his mouth to put his two cents in and I know what he's going to say. "It's not out of the question. Just...not right now."

"That makes sense," he nods.

Both of us are quiet. What do people even talk about on dates that won't bore the other person to tears? I'm not sure what the hell Stella was thinking when setting this date up. Especially without my knowledge. He's not even the type of guy I'd go for. For fuck's sake, I was practically raised in this bar by my uncle. This man looks like he doesn't have one scrap of ink on him. I take a peek at his clothes, and he looks like he's defined. But he doesn't have the arm porn I'm used to seeing on some of the crowd that used to come here.

"Look at you two hitting it off." She's way too excited about something that isn't happening. "I just knew you'd be great for each other." Stella swoops to the end of the bar, standing beside me with her elbows propped on the countertop, chin resting on her hands. She looks like a modern-day cupid. The only thing she's missing are the wings and bow and arrow.

"Hey, Stella." My date waves half-heartedly. Clearly, we aren't hitting it off. Too bad my friend can't seem to see it.

"Hi, Roger." She grins before raising a hand to signal one of the bartenders. Yes, Roger, that's his name. "What are y'all talking about?"

Before Roger can say anything, I stand from my barstool. I've given this long enough, and now that she's seen I tried, maybe she'll back off for a bit. "Can I talk to you for a sec?"

"Sure." Stella straightens.

"In the office?" I head down the hall, past the bathroom, to the closed door at the end. There's no need to check behind me. I know she's following. Curiosity must be killing her.

Taking my place in the chair behind the desk, I push aside the papers to see the desk calendar. In tiny print the words "Roger - lunch date" are written in the square. Nice way to cover her ass.

Stella closes the door softly behind her before facing me. "Why did you leave—"

I raise my hand. "Don't even go there, Stell."

"Go where? I thought the two of you were having a great time."

Deep breath in and out. "No. He's the complete opposite of me in every way. Besides, I was working. You've got to stop springing these dates on me. It's not fair to me or whatever unsuspecting man you have meeting me up here."

Her eyes are wide, and I feel like shit for going off on her. But this has to stop. "I'm just trying to help you find someone."

I lift my hand to my forehead and smooth out the wrinkles I'm sure are forming. "I know, but I'm fine, Stella. I'm not looking for a relationship right now. Hell, I don't even have time for one. The bar takes up every second I have of every day. It's even worse when we have people calling out. Being part of a couple just isn't high on my priority list."

She crosses her arms over her chest and glares at me. "First, you need a manager and possibly an assistant manager. We'll hold a job fair to get more people on the payroll. That should free up some time for you." I want to scream, that's not the point, but she won't listen. "Not necessarily for dating. But for going out and having fun. To do something for you besides the bar. We've got everything set up for success. We just need a few more dependable employees."

"True. We'll call a staff meeting for this weekend and schedule the job fair." She had a lot of success when she was opening up the distribution center, and I know she'll do amazing with this because she truly cares about how well this bar does.

"Sounds good," she nods and sits down in the chair in front of me desk. "I also have an idea."

I don't know if I should be scared or not. The last time

she told me she had an idea we did a complete remodel of this place. There's no telling what she has brewing in her head now.

2

dylan

RAIN IS POURING on the windshield and lightning flashes in the distance as I slow down to keep from hitting the car in front of me. I swear, a little bit of rain and everyone on the highway suddenly forgets how to drive. It doesn't help that I'm not the most excited about my destination. Never in a million years did I think I would end up back in Asheville after a few short years away. If it were up to me, it'd be another decade before I stepped foot in that town, minimum.

Theoretically it's not a bad place to live. My childhood wasn't horrible. My teen years weren't either, for that matter. But when you're faced with the same people in the dating pool and having to pick sides because one friend broke up with another, it's an entirely different thing. If I would have stayed, my soul would have died piece by piece.

I don't have a choice about going back now, though. My mom needs me. After all the years she kept me out of trouble and a path of success, I can't let her down. She deserves more than that. Being a single mom wasn't easy on her. She was always exhausted and there were nights I didn't see her until almost midnight because she was picking up extra shifts to pay for football or whatever else I needed. Now it's my turn to repay her. To take care of her the way she always did for me.

The car in front of me hits a patch of high water and I press on my brakes, waiting to see if this driver knows what they're doing or if they are going to end up with the hood of their car smashed into the sidewall. It veers closer and closer to the cement wall, but they correct the trajectory and manage to get back in the lane. Thank God. I would have stopped to help if there was a wreck, but this isn't the ideal weather to do that. It'd put me and them in danger of getting side swiped by one of these idiots not paying attention.

The right lane is comfortable for going slower, but the tilt of the road means all the water piles up there. I turn on my blinker and wait thirty seconds before moving into the middle lane. My car rumbles as I press the gas pedal. The sooner I get to Asheville the sooner I get out of this hellacious rain. Next time I'll check the forecast before heading home. It would save myself some frustration. As much as I don't want to go back, I prefer that than driving with these assholes surrounding me. Let's just hope it's not the shit-show I left behind.

* * *

Fuck. The rain was pounding so hard and kept my attention on the road that I wasn't paying attention to my gas gauge. My car is sputtering as I take the exit for Asheville. Lucky for me, there's a gas station right around the corner. It's a good thing I know this town like the back of my hand. And the car, too. It's an old Camero I've been fixing up since I left Asheville. One part at a time. The line is creeping closer to the orange but I don't trust it to get even lower. The likelihood of being stranded on the side of the road grows as the needle makes its way down.

Rolling into the gas station, I park next to the closest pump. The rain is still coming down. Not as hard, but enough to be annoying. I lift the center console and pull my wallet out. Opening the car door, I step outside, pull my card out of my wallet and lift my hand to slide the card into the pump. There's a piece of tape over the slot. Could this night get any worse? I just want to go home, see what my mom needs, and see how long I'm going to be stuck in this town. If anything, maybe I can get her to move. It wouldn't be horrible to have her down the road from me. She'd have whatever help she needs and we can both get out of here.

Cynical? Maybe, but I didn't exactly leave everything hunky dory when I bailed that summer. The drama of Jake and Tonya was too much. There was no chance he and Tonya were ever going to get back together and be a happy little family. But no, he had to punch Randall for no damn reason. It was the last straw. I couldn't still be friends with Jake and Tonya, and keep my own sanity. I'm not sure how Marshall did it. He has a lot more patience than I do.

Closing the car door, I run through the slowing rain to the gas station door. "Hey," I say to the cashier. "Can I get twenty on the pump at the end?"

"Sure thing." He rings up my total and I add a pack of gum to the counter.

I'm sliding the card through the machine when I hear a voice behind me. "Holy shit." Great. Speak of the devil. "I didn't know you were coming back to town. When did you get in?"

The urge to ignore him is strong, but I suck it up and turn toward him. "Hey, man. I actually just rolled in." Literally. It's like thinking about him conjured him up.

"That's awesome. I was just about to meet Marshall and the rest of the gang at the bar." He pauses for a second to see if I'll say anything. "You should come with. I'm sure they'll be excited to see you."

"I don't know." The indecision is clear in my voice. I mean, it might be nice to see everyone again. Or...it might be a fucking disaster and everyone will start fighting like old times. You never know with these guys. The cashier is looking at us like we're ping pong balls on a table. Eyes bouncing to me and then him. "I'm heading home. The drive was nothing short of hellacious."

"Oh." Jake's shoulders sag and he looks like I just kicked his puppy. "Well, if you change your mind, we'll be at Out of the Ashes."

Wow. That place is still open. It was falling apart when I left town and hardly anyone went there. Well, except the bikers that came around after the owner passed away. I wasn't old enough to be in there at the time so I never tried to see what the inside looked like. I may have acted like your typical high school party boy, but I followed the rules. Well, most of them.

"I'll keep that in mind." I stick my hand out to shake his hand before I walk out the door. But he bypasses that completely and gives me a weird one-armed hug. This is awkward as fuck. "Well," I say disentangling myself from him. "I better get some gas in my car before I screw it up."

"Oh, yeah," he backs away from me. "It was good to see

you and I hope you stop by. A lot has changed since you've been gone."

"I might see you there." Walking out the door, I head to the gas pump and fill up my car. It's a cool Spring night and I wish I had some sort of jacket in my backseat. It's in a suitcase in the trunk and I could pull it out, but I don't feel like it. Jake leaves the gas station and waves as he heads to his truck. Well, that hasn't changed. He's still driving that gas guzzling thing. Not that I can say much. This car looks badass, but the mileage is horrific.

The gas pump clicks off and I put the nozzle back in its holder. My baby roars to life as I put the key in the ignition and turn. It's a sound I've always loved. It's a wonder I never decided to race cars for a living. I'm still young enough that I could, but there's no passion there for me.

The sky is pitch black with lightning flashing in the distance. The storm moving on to another destination. I pull out of the gas station and turn right toward town and my house. New housing developments are being built on both sides of the road and I can't believe this place is actually growing. All I wanted was to get away from this place, and people want to come here. It's mind-blowing. I wonder if they know how boring it really is here.

Great. A red light at one of the few lights we actually have in town. Everything looks the same but different. I'm not sure if it's because it's night and I haven't been here in years, or if it's because I'm looking at it through a different lens. Either way, I'm not sure how I feel about being back here, aside from not really wanting to. Instead of turning left to head to my mom's house, I go right. Without even thinking about it, my subconscious is taking me to Out of the Ashes. I'm either a masochist that likes to see a train wreck, or curious to see exactly how much has changed in the years I've been gone. I only hope I don't regret it.

* * *

This. This place is nothing like I remember. For one there's a bright neon sign sitting in the front. And there's a fucking line to get in. When did that happen? When I was a teen, there was never a full parking lot. I was lucky to find a space in the lot without having to park somewhere else and walk.

I bypass the line and stop at the host stand. The short girl standing behind it holds her hand up. "You'll have to go to the back of the line."

"Um," I scratch my head. This is my out. A sign for me to take my ass home and check in on my mom. I catch a glimpse of Jake through the window. And holy shit. Tonya is sitting at the table with him. Along with the rest of our old crew and a few faces I don't know. "Actually, Jake told me to meet him here."

"Oh," she beams. "You must be Dylan. I'll lead you to his table."

Well, the decision is made, I need to find out exactly what brought on these changes. Especially one so drastic Tonya and Jake are within breathing space of each other. Tonight, may end up being a disaster, but at least I'll learn the scoop about what's been going on since I've been gone.

3

angie

THE JOB FAIR can't come soon enough. I really need more people here to help me manage nights like tonight. Weeknights are usually fine. A couple of people can do it if they are busting ass, but the weekends...that's a whole other ballpark. It's all hands-on deck. The tables are full, some people are standing in corners by the bar, and the line outside is growing by the minute.

It doesn't help that the kids I used to babysit are taking up one of my biggest tables. I can't begrudge them it, though. They rarely have a chance to get out and do anything together with growing families and crazy work schedules. Marshall's girlfriend's schedule is as bad as mine. I have a sneaking suspicion she's just as much of a workaholic as me, too. She definitely picked a good one to be with. He's one of the few from that group that had a level head even as a kid.

Lisa is leading a tall, muscular guy to their table. I'm

not sure who he is because I can't see his face, but from the back...I like what I'm seeing. A woman in front of me waves her hand. "Excuse me, can I get a vodka tonic?"

I don't see how anyone can drink those, but it's not my job to judge others. "Sure, thing." Reaching to the side, I grab a short glass, toss in some ice cubes, and glance for the bottle of vodka. All while keeping an eye on the newcomer. Even though I can't see his face, and he's never come in before.

The motions are autopilot when making drinks. It doesn't take much thought. Not the way it did when I started bartending here all those years ago. With the drink finished, I lift it up to give to the customer. "Here you g—." The words die on my lips and the glass slips from my hand, shattering on the edge of the counter. There's no way in hell. Dylan is who I would babysit on a regular basis. His mom was always working, and I'd take him to his little league practices. I did everything I could to help them out because I knew they were struggling. But damn...he grew up.

"Shit." The woman who ordered the drink yells.

My cheeks flame red. "Crap, I'm so sorry. Did anything get on you?" I completely spaced out when I saw him and forgot about this woman's now non-existent drink.

She looks down to check her clothes. "No, I don't think so."

"Good. I'll have Carlos make you another drink and I'll get whatever you've had on your tab since you've been here." Jesus. An attractive guy walks in, one I used to fucking babysit, and I lose all capability of making a simple drink.

"You don't have to do that." She waves me away. "Another drink would be great, though."

I feel like a complete moron. I haven't broken a glass since I first started bartending. That was years ago when I began working here to pay for college. Too bad for this customer, though. I'm still going to pay her tab. I mean, it was my fuck up.

Waving at Carlos from across the counter, he meets me halfway. "Can you make her another vodka tonic while I get this mess cleaned up?"

"Sure thing." He stops beside me on his way to remake the drink. "What happened? I don't think I've ever seen you spill a drink, much less break a glass."

Because I don't. Ever. "I got distracted." Dylan has joined his old group at their table.

Carlos follows my gaze. "I can see why."

Damn it. I'm going to get shit for this for a long time. I can already tell. The whispers will start tonight during clean up and the story will transform by morning. "Shut up." I turn toward him. "Oh, can you also find out what name her tab is under so I can take care of it?"

"Yep." He points to the other end of the bar. "That's the broom. Try not to get too distracted on the way to get it." He rushes off before I can say anything else. I swear sometimes the people I employ can be jerks.

Grabbing the broom, I walk back to where the accident happened. The end of the broom somehow hits Carlos in the arm. Oops. His shoulders shake in laughter, but he doesn't make a sound. One day I'll get him back.

Now that the mess is swept up, I can get around to doing actual work things. I'm dumping the glass in the trash can when I hear Jake at the bar counter. "Hey Ang, you'll never believe who is back in town." He sounds like a child who was given their favorite toy. There's way too much excitement. "Angie, are you listening to me?"

That question is what stops me in my tracks. Not because I'm not listening, but because it was something he always said when I babysat him. His parents never listened to him. Thank God he got away from those crazies. I just don't ever want him to think I won't listen. Even now as an adult with a family of his own.

"Yes, Jake, I'm listening." As big as his ego is, he still wants to be heard. "I was cleaning up a mess I made."

"Oh, sorry." It's crazy seeing all these kids I used to babysit in the bar. A small part of me wants to chastise them, but then I remember they are grown and it makes me feel older than I am. "Anyway, come to the table when you get a sec. We have a surprise for you."

As if I didn't notice him walk into my bar. I notice everything that happens here. Like the two guys arguing at one of the corner tables. It's not an issue right now, but I'll be keeping an eye on them. "Give me a few minutes and I'll be over there."

"You're gonna flip." With those parting words, he rushes back to their table.

It's a good thing he didn't see my reaction when Dylan walked through the door. He'd never let me live it down. Much like I'm sure my employees won't.

With the broom in hand, I make my way from around the bar, down the hall and to my office. A few minutes. That's all I need to compose myself. There's no way in hell I can let on to any of them that I've had any sort of reaction. I used to babysit him for crying out loud. Attraction isn't something I should be feeling. But just in case, I check my reflection in the mirror. Not only to make sure my hair isn't going crazy, but to see if I spilled any of the vodka on my shirt when I dropped the drink.

There are a couple of wet spots, and I turn to the makeshift closet we built into the office. Every employee keeps an extra shirt or two in here just in case. You honestly never know what's going to happen on a day-to-day basis. I pull one of my white Out of the Ashes shirts from the shelf and set it on the desk. Lifting the bottom of my dirty shirt, I pull it up. It's halfway up when the office door opens, and I freeze. "Hey boss," Carlos says seconds before he sees me. "Oh my god. Why don't you have a shirt on?"

I shove my hands down. So much for changing. "What the hell are you doing in here? Who's watching the bar?" He's literally the only bartender I have on schedule tonight other than me.

"Dude, everything out there is fine. The line has slowed down a bit and Lisa is keeping an eye on things from the stand."

"Okay, that doesn't explain what you're doing back here."

"I wanted to make sure you're okay. You seemed a little spaced out." He jerks his thumb toward the door. "I'll just leave you to yourself and go back to the bar."

Ugh. Now I feel like an asshole. He was being a good friend and employee. There aren't many companies that have such a close-knit community and aren't related. I trust both Carlos and Lisa with everything I have. If only I could find more employees like them. "No, I'm sorry. I'm not myself."

"Want to talk about it?" He leans against the wall waiting to see if I'll talk. It's not a bad idea. Stella knows most of my concerns. Especially with the ideas she has about growing this place even bigger than we already have.

"Yes, but not right now." I forget about the clean shirt,

and head toward him and the door. "We still have three hours until closing time. We need to be out there more than ever. You know how some of these people get after a few too many drinks."

"If that ain't the truth," he laughs. He moves to the side to let me pass in front of him. "After you." Before I'm all the way through, he touches my arm. "Tonight, though, we talk. Once we kick everyone out, we're going to have a drink and get to the bottom of what's bothering you."

"There's no way out of it?" Please say yes.

"Nope," he shakes his head. "How are we going to find more people to work if you're always stressed?"

He has a point. Right now, there's no other way to be than stressed. We move two steps forward and one step back, and if I implement the changes Stella is talking about, I'll need people I can rely on. The four of us can't keep this place afloat alone. Well, three of us. Stella is more the creative thinker and we get shit done. Which isn't a bad thing. Even now, this is more than my uncle ever dreamed it could be. Would he be proud of the direction the bar has taken, though? I sure as hell hope so.

"You're right. Let's get out there before sweet little Lisa loses her shit on everyone." She's sweet as candy, but if someone riles her up, she'll let them have it without a second thought.

We walk out of the office just in time to see Lisa marching toward us. Oh great. This can't be good. "Y'all need to get out here. There are people in front of the bar waiting for a drink, and I can't serve them because I'm not certified to do it." Lisa swings her long hair over her shoulder and marches right back to the front of the bar to the comfort of her stand.

"We better go." We come out of the hallways and Lisa

may have exaggerated a tiny bit. There are around four people waiting for someone to refill their drink. She made it sound like there was a hoard of people. "You take the far end and I'll take this one."

"Got it," Carlos nods. "After that, go see what Jake wanted."

I mock salute him and take the first order. Less than five minutes. That's all it takes for me to get caught up on the refills on my side of the bar. With everyone's glasses full, I wipe down the bar and walk around to the opening. It's time to let Jake think he's surprising me with Dylan's return.

The path to get to them isn't easy to get through. Groups of friends are yelling at each other to be heard over the music. Or, maybe, they are feeling the alcohol and don't realize how loud they are. Pushing through people, I'm almost to Jake when the two guys from earlier can be heard hollering at each other. Time to nip this in the bud. I'm not going to let these two idiots ruin everyone else's night.

My feet lead me right past Jake's table and to the two arguing. Uncle Max always worried when I threw myself between two men in a predicament, but I've never had too much trouble. They usually see little ol' me step between them and cool it. I hope like hell it happens with these two. "Guys, I'm going to need y'all to chill."

They keep yelling over me and don't acknowledge my presence. Oh hell no. I will not be ignored in my own bar. This time I throw my hands out so I've got one on each guy. That stops them, temporarily. "If you don't stop yelling at each other, you need to leave. I don't care what you do outside those doors, but I will not allow this in my bar."

For a second, I think I've gotten through to them, but it's short lived. The guy on my right throws a punch. Not at me, but over my head. The other one defends himself and my uncle's worst nightmare comes true. I'm in the middle of a fight because these assholes have lost their damn minds. I try to get out from between them but an elbow catches me in the face and I go down.

4

dylan

WHAT THE ACTUAL fuck is Angie thinking? As soon as one of the guys throws a punch, I'm out of my chair. Who the hell throws a punch when there's a woman standing between him and the person he is fighting? And, the other guy takes a swing in response? These two seem to lack some home training. My feet lead me straight toward Angie, and I push the two assholes to the side to get to her.

You would think what would be the end of their fight. I mean, it would be for anybody else. But, no, not for these two idiots. They are dead set on killing each other regardless of who gets hurt in the aftermath. Guys like these are the reason I wanted to stay out of this small ass town. It seems like no matter what, there is drama in every corner.

Lucky for me, even after all this time, my friends have my back. Randall and Jake are on either side of me, each with a man in their possession. And, of course, these two are still trying to get at each other. It kind of makes me wonder what they were fighting about that is so important, but the red mark on Angie's face makes me decide I really don't give a fuck.

"Angie," I've bent down next to her on the floor so she can hear me. Although, that shouldn't be a problem because the entire bar has gone eerily silent. "Are you okay?"

She tries sitting up and loses her balance. I throw my arm out behind her to catch her before she hits the floor again. "I think so." The dazed look in her eyes tells me otherwise. "I know for a fact my brother and I used to get into fights and even when he knocked me to the ground, I don't think I've ever felt like this."

"No offense, but your brother also wasn't two hundred fifty pounds when you were duking it out in your backyard." At least she's making jokes. It makes me feel a little bit better about how she's going to hold up later on. I glance up at Jake and Randall, "you got them?"

"Yeah," Jake nods. "What do you want us to do with them? Throw them outside? Call the cops? Beat their asses?"

In all honesty, I'm good with option three. It's what they deserve after getting Angie mixed up in their squabble. I look down at Ang and raise an eyebrow. "What do you want to do?"

She rubs the back of her head and winces. "Throw them out. And make sure they understand they are banned from Out of the Ashes, no exceptions."

"You heard her." Since my arm is already around her back, I use my free arm and place it beneath her knees, picking her up and carrying her to our table.

"Oh my God, put me down." She bats at my chest. "They knocked me down and nothing more. I'm perfectly capable of walking."

It takes everything in me not to laugh. "I don't know, it

looks like you hit the floor pretty hard. And I don't want to see anything happen to you on my watch."

She snorts then grabs her head, groaning. "What do you mean on your watch? This is the first time you've been back in years."

So, she's noticed my absence. Not that I expected her to keep tabs on me, but the sentiment is nice. Especially when I had the biggest crush on her as a kid. I figured when she went to school, she forgot all about us kids she used to look out for. Honestly, I probably wouldn't have been involved in sports if it wasn't for her. It's hard to get where you need to be when your single mom is working all the time to put food on the table. She was my transportation.

"And your point? I'm here now." I set her in the chair I almost toppled over when I went to rescue her ass.

"Angie," a short guy rushes to the table. I think he may be one of the bartenders, though I can't be sure because like she pointed out, I haven't been home in years. "Are you okay?"

"Yeah, I'm fine. Nothing a little ice and pain meds won't fix." She tries to wave away the towel he pushes toward the back of her head. It's chunky, and I assume filled with ice.

"Or, you could have a concussion," I grunt. "You should probably get checked out to make sure."

She finally relents and grabs the towel of ice and presses it to her head. "I will after we close. We're short staffed in case you haven't noticed."

"I'm sure this guy can run things." I point my thumb toward the guy that came over. "You aren't going to be much good around here if you don't take care of yourself." If there's one thing I've learned growing up here, it's that.

It's also why I think my mom has the health issues she does. She never took time out to make sure she was okay.

"This guy has a name." The man next to me stares me down. "It's Carlos."

"Well, nice to meet you, Carlos." I thrust out my hand for him to shake, but he only eyes me. Like I might become a problem instead of the two assholes that caused the scene. I'm obviously not going to win any brownie points with him. A part of me wonders if him and Angie have anything going on. Not that it's any of my business. I can't let my childhood crush get the best of me. It's not like I'll be here for long.

Realizing he isn't going to shake my hand, I put it in my pocket. The rejection stings, but to him I'm an outsider. My old group of friends aren't. He's not going to pay me any mind. "He's right," Carlos finally says. "You should get checked out. Lisa and I can handle things. The mood of the bar isn't quite what it was about thirty minutes ago." Good, so he's noticed the diminishing crowd as well.

She looks around the emptying room and sighs. "I guess I can't argue with that." She stands up, sways a bit, and grabs the edge of the table for balance.

"Are you okay?" Tonya tries to whisper. It's loud considering she has to be heard over the music still blasting through the speakers.

"Just a little dizzy."

Tonya stands and grabs hold of Angie's arm. "Here, I'll take you to the emergency room. You definitely don't need to be driving if you can barely stand."

"I can take her." I hold my hand out again.

"It's okay, Dylan," Angie says. "Tonya can take me."

"Oh yeah, sure." Not going to lie. The rejection stings. Though I'm not sure what I expected. It's been years since

I've been around anyone in this room. Any trips I've made home to visit my mom, I've managed to keep quiet. I was like a ghost in my home town. But seeing how my friends have grown up. In relationships, and having families of their own, I can't help but feel like I've missed out on so much. As much as I felt like I was always on the edge of the group when we were teenagers, I might as well be on another continent now. I should have gone straight home after bumping into Jake. Coming here was a mistake.

Tonya whispers something to her husband, and leads Angie toward the front door. I watch them through the window until I see them get into a car. Tapping my knuckles on the table, I look around at my high school friends. "I'm going to head home."

Jake gasps. "What? No, stay for a while longer. We didn't even get to have a whole beer together."

"We'll catch up before I leave. I need to get home to my mom." It's mostly true. I do need to go home, but Angie rejecting my offer to take her to get checked out still hurts.

"Sure," Jake mumbles. He seems like a completely different person than the one I left behind. I'm happy for him, but I can't come back like nothing ever happened. Like he didn't try to fight one of his best friends over a long-ago crush. The smalltown drama is something I don't miss at all.

Waving to the table in general, I head toward the front door. The hostess is still standing behind the stand even though there is no longer a line. I guess a fight brings the whole mood down. I take a peek out the door, checking if the losers Jake threw out are still hanging out in the parking lot. Even if Ang did refuse my help, I can't help but wonder if this is a common occurrence. It doesn't sit well with me that it might be.

Instead of leaving, I head back to the bar. Carlos is cleaning a glass when he sees me approach. "Sorry about earlier, man. Angie was my first concern."

A flare of jealousy burns through me. Does that concern go further than that of a boss and employee? I have no right to be pissed, but I can't help it. I'm also not going to ask. My old feelings need to go back to being buried. "It's all good. Does that happen often?" I point my thumb behind me to indicate the fight.

He shrugs. "Not really." Setting the glass down, he leans forward on the bar. "We get the occasional arguments, but it never escalated to fists. Though, lately, it seems like we are getting more and more cocky kids that think they don't have to follow the rules. It wasn't this bad before. At least, not until the rebrand. It brings in a younger crowd and while most of them are fine some of them act like they have no manners. With the upgrades Stella is wanting to pitch to Angie, I don't see it getting any better in the future."

"What changes?"

"It's not really my place to say." He picks up another glass since the bar is empty aside from one man at the end of the bar, sipping on his beer. "But think bigger."

"If this place continues to grow, you're going to need some sort of security."

Carlos laughs. "I've brought it up to Angie before, but she doesn't think we need it. According to her, she can handle anything that walks through that door."

"Yeah, she did a real good job dealing with them tonight."

"If you've known her for any length of time, you know just how stubborn she is." He's right. She has been since I've known her. She gave me a run for my money. My mom would give in to my rebellion when I was younger. Not

Angie, she would wait me out. And as much as I thought she was hot, it was annoying as hell.

"Maybe if she hears it from someone else, after tonight, she'll listen."

"Good luck."

"Take it easy," I call behind me as I walk to the door. I think I know what I'll propose to Angie when I see her again. With the bar taking off the way it has, she's only going to attract more of that craziness. She needs someone around to handle it. And I need a job to help pay for my mom's medical bills. It'll be a win-win situation.

5

angie

THE ROOM the nurse put me in is quiet. Doors opening and closing down the hall are the only things that can be heard. This table thing is uncomfortable and the paper rolled across the top crinkles with every shift of my body.

"Why are you moving around so much?" Tonya is sitting in a chair at the end of the bed. Table? I don't know what it should be called. She could have waited in the car, but talked me into letting her come in. No doubt it's to make sure I actually get checked out.

"Between being here and you studying me like I'm a specimen under a microscope, it's weird. I can't help but try to get comfy." Another crinkly as I move to pull my phone out of my back pocket.

"I'm not studying you," she crosses her arms and stares me down. "I just want to make sure you're okay. You work yourself way harder than you should."

She's right on that front, but it's a bullshit excuse. "No, you are in here because you're worried. You keep looking at me like that because you have something to say. You just haven't figured out the right wording, yet." I raise an eyebrow, waiting for her to argue.

After a few moments of silence, she uncrosses her arms. "You're right, but how did you know that?"

"I used to babysit you. I know all your tells. Growing up didn't mean they magically went away."

Tonya opens her mouth and is interrupted by the handle turning. The doctor comes into the room. "How are we doing tonight, Miss Donovan?" He realizes Tonya is in the room and backtracks. "I'm sorry, I didn't see you there. Maybe Miss isn't the right word?"

I'm barely holding in my laughter while I wait for Tonya to understand his meaning. I mean, it's not a stretch. She probably knows me the best. She stuck around after high school and saw my struggle with the bar. I ran into her at Brews Clues more times than I can count. Who knew someone so much younger than me could be the shoulder I would lean on?

When she finally catches what he's saying, she waves her hands around. "No, we're just friends and I had to make sure she actually got checked out and didn't kill time until she thought it was appropriate to come back to the car." She makes it sound like I'm a teenage delinquent. As if her group of friends didn't do some shady shit when they were teens. But I'll let it slide. She did bring me here so I wouldn't be in the same car as Dylan. Not that it matters.

"Oh," the doctor laughs. "I didn't want to assume, or offend. Apologies." He glances at me. "Are you okay with your friend staying in the room?"

I lean closer to see what his name tag says. "Yep, Doc Boone. If not, I'll just have to tell her everything when I walk out."

"Okay," he claps his hands, and the sound sends a dull thud through my head. "What are you in for tonight?"

I set my phone down beside me, and sit up straight. I don't know why I feel like I have to have great posture when I'm around an authority figure. "I, um, fell at work and hit my head." I rub the bump forming to drive the point home.

"That is not at all how it went down," Tonya jumps from her seat.

Doctor Boone turns his attention to her. "And what happened that she's leaving out?" He glances toward me to see if I'll answer. Not gonna happen.

"So, she owns Out of the Ashes and these two guys started getting rowdy. Instead of doing something smart, like calling the cops, she gets in between them to try to calm them down. Well, punches are thrown and she gets hit before falling and hitting her head." Good grief. She didn't have to make it sound like a bigger deal than it was.

"So," the doctor pulls something out of the pocket of his jacket. "You were hit and hit your head?"

"Yes," I grumble. Why do I feel like I did something wrong when I was trying to keep all of my other patrons safe?

"Where were you hit?"

"I'm not sure." When he raises his eyebrows, I shake my head, instantly regretting it. "It wasn't on my face. I think one of them clipped my arm and that's when I lost my balance."

He clicks a small pen-like tool and the end shines bright. "Okay, I need you to follow the light with your eyes." He moves it from left to right then up and down. "That looks good. Now, where did you hit your head? I need to check the bump I'm sure you have."

Sliding my hand over my head, I stop on the bump that feels like it's the size of a baseball. I really hope it's not that big. I won't be able to wear my hair up for days. "It's right here."

He touches the spot and I wince. It hurts and as much as I like to pretend I'm tough, tears spring to my eyes. "Can you look down?" I do as he asks and can feel my hair shift as he tries for a closer look. "Well, Miss Donovan, you have a decent size bump. The plus side is it is swelling out instead of in. Do you have a headache or any other pain?"

"Yes, it's not bad. Just annoying." That's the only way I can describe it.

"The good news is I don't think you have a concussion. You remember the events that happened and you seem to be coherent. But I would pay attention to anything else that may pop up in the next few days. If you start feeling sluggish, or confused, come back so we can take another look." He pauses to make sure I understand everything he said. "Not that it's any of my business, but I do hope you press charges against the two brawlers."

Tonya snorts, but doesn't add anything. "I'll keep that in mind. Thank you, Doc. It's a relief that I'm cleared to go back to work."

"Just...take it easy."

"I will." Another snort can be heard from behind the doctor. "Thank you for seeing me."

"That's why I'm here," he smiles. "I'll leave the paperwork with the receptionist. Stop by her desk before you leave."

"Will do."

He gives a slight wave and exits the room as fast as he came in. "You are the worst liar I've ever seen." Tonya stands next to me with her hand out to help me up.

I wave her off and slide off the table. "I don't know what you're talking about?"

She follows me to the door. "You aren't going to take it easy tomorrow. You will take on all the responsibilities at the bar like you normally do. You really need to work on your staffing problem."

"Are you volunteering?" I grab the handle and turn. "I can't exactly delegate when I can't keep employees. All of them keep moving off to bigger and better things. Not that I blame them, but every time we seem to have everything under control, someone quits."

I'm met with silence. She walks past me and out the door. No doubt going to the car. It's fine, I don't need her to be with me to pay for the visit. After a few quick words and handing over my debit card, the bill is taken care of and I'm free to go home. Hurrying out of the clinic, I open the door and slide into the passenger seat. "I'm sorry. I didn't mean to blow up on you."

"It's all good. I get it." She starts the car and turns the lights on. The light almost blinding as it reflects off the clinic windows. "You need to talk with Stella and have her do the job fair sooner rather than later. And all plans she has for the stage need to be halted until the staffing issue is resolved."

She's not wrong, but the last sentence catches me off guard. "Wait, how did you know about the stage area? I haven't told anyone about that, not even my parents."

She grins and it's mischievous under the lamp lights as she backs out and gets us on the road. "You forget, Reaf and

Johnny are buddies. Johnny can't keep a secret to save his life." Which means the whole town knows. Great.

Why is she always right? "Remind me to tell Stella not to divulge our secrets to her husband." I shake my head, wondering how far word has gotten. "And the job fair is first on my list. I need dependable people. You'd think that wouldn't be hard considering we have a junior college in town. Surely those kids need an income."

"They do," Tonya shrugs. "You just have to make it enticing for them."

Good grief. "I guess I'll spend the rest of the night thinking of ways to do that."

"No," Tonya shakes her head. "You are going to go home, go to bed, and let Stella handle it. That's literally her job." When I don't reply, she slows the car down. "Don't make me take you to my place and force you into bed. Layla is all for sleepovers but she won't be happy to find you in hers when she gets home from my parents' house."

As cute as that kid is, she's definitely stubborn. With my luck, she'd roll me out, or jump on me until I wake up. "Okay, I'll go to bed."

"Good." We're minutes away from home when she asks, "So what was up with your reaction to Dylan tonight?"

"Oh no. I may have promised to go to bed, but I'm nixing that conversation." There's no way in hell I'm going to admit I find him attractive to one of the people he grew up with. Especially not when I'm the one that looked after them most of the time.

"I'll let it slide...for now." She parks in my driveway and waits for me to open the door. "But I expect answers tomorrow."

I jump out of the car before she can lock me in. "You'll

be waiting for a long time, T." She laughs as I close the door and make way to the porch. Digging my key out of my bag, I take a few seconds to breathe. All of today's problems will be there tomorrow. I open the front door and close it behind me. All I want right now is my bed and a decent night's sleep.

6

dylan

THE HOUSE WAS dark when I got home last night. I assumed Mom was in her bedroom since it was so late and my energy was still buzzing from throwing those assholes out of Angie's bar last night. I'm still mulling over the issue she's having with rowdy patrons when I walk into the living room and stop in my tracks.

Mom is lying on the couch with her cast bound foot set on top of a pile of pillows. She must have fallen asleep waiting on me to come home. Now...I feel like shit for going to the bar first. Even though part of me wonders what would have happened had I not been there. I'm sure Jake, Marshall, and Randall would have taken care of it, but it's not the same as me being there. I don't have anyone to look out for. They have girlfriends and wives to lookout for and their reaction wouldn't have been as fast as mine. The fact that I had a crush on her throughout my teen years holds no bearing.

Mom shifts and I know I need to do something since

I've proven to be a shitty son by not coming straight here last night. But I don't want to wake her up. Not yet. Breakfast is the answer. She'll wake up on her own when she smells the bacon.

My phone dings from my pocket as I'm walking into the kitchen. I pull it out as I open the fridge to take stock of what she has. I'm sure I'll have to get groceries at some point.

JAKE

We all had fun last night. The guys are going to hit some golf balls. You in?

This is what I was afraid of when I went to the bar last night. We'd fall into old patterns and I would be the odd man out. Again. Things wouldn't be different now either. Every single person I hung out with then is in a relationship now. I shouldn't take so much stock in that but I don't have their same shared experiences. Hell, that was part of the reason I never came back after I left. Being put in the middle and having to pick sides isn't something anyone should have to do with the people they've grown up with.

I don't want to reject the offer right away, even though I'm going to decline. I set my phone on the counter and pull out everything I need. It's weird holding these things. They are a relic from my childhood. A memory of all the time I made myself dinner because Mom was holding down two jobs to support me and my hobbies. I'd like to say playing football got me somewhere, but it didn't. At least, not for long.

I set the pan on the stove and turn on the burner waiting for it to heat up before adding the eggs. The sausage is already formed into patties and I put them in the other pan. I'm bummed there's not bacon, but I'll work with what she has.

There's nothing quite like being in your childhood home, questioning everything about your life.

"I see you finally made it home," Mom calls out.

"Technically, you can't see me, Mom." There's a wall between where the stove is and where she's at on the couch. Even if she craned her neck, she wouldn't be able to see me.

"Don't be a smart aleck, Dylan." The laugh at the end is the only indication she's playing. She had a much different tone when I would pop off as a teenager. I'll never admit I deserved it, though. "Are you cooking breakfast?"

Yet another chance for me to be a smart ass, but I'll refrain. This is the first time I've seen her in almost a year and it's only to help her out while she's in a cast. "Yep. You were out of bacon so it's eggs and sausage. I'll have to go grocery shopping at some point today." I noticed how bare her fridge is and I can't let that stand while I'm here. It's only her here, but she should have other options. Maybe when I leave, I'll sign her up for one of those meal services.

"Well, it smells and sounds delicious." She's quiet for a few moments and I assumed she's dozed off again. But something hits the floor hard. My heart pounds as I turn off the burners and rush to the living room, expecting to see that she's fallen on the floor. It was just a cup, though. A wet spot has formed on the carpet beside the coffee table and I breathe a sigh of relief. "Why on earth are you breathing so hard?"

She's staring at me like I've lost my mind. "Because I thought you fell." It takes everything in my power to keep my voice calm and not like I'm in the middle of a freak out. "You should call for me when you need my help. That's the entire reason I'm here."

She points at the blanket and cup. "When I threw the blanket off, it hit the cup and made it fall. I'm fine. Besides, I've managed to get around on my own all this time without you here."

"That's before you were in a cast," I mutter.

"Don't sass me," she wags her finger at me. "You didn't have to come out here to take care of me. I never asked you to do that. You have an entire life and don't have to hit pause because I fell and broke my leg."

"And how exactly are you planning on working while in that thing? I'm here to make things easier for you. It's the least I can do after everything you've done for me my entire life." Why does she have to turn this into an argument? She's so freaking stubborn. But, if anything ever happened to her, I'd be completely alone, and I'm not ready for that. I don't know that I'll ever be.

She pats the couch next to her, and I sit down. "I appreciate it. I really do. This is just a bump in the road. It may take me a little longer to clean houses, but I can handle it." She scratches the back of her neck and I know she's lying. Or, at the very least, keeping something from me. It's one of her tells, but I'll let it slide for now.

"Well, while I'm here you don't have to worry about that. Surely, they aren't expecting you to come back to work within days of getting your cast." Yes, I'm fishing for information. I won't apologize for it, though.

"No, I've got some time off." Way to be specific there, Mom.

"Then I'm here for whatever time you have off." I move

the blanket and fold it up before grabbing the cup. I'll have to get a towel to soak up the water. "Make a list of everything you need done around here, and I'll make sure it all gets done."

"What about your work?"

"I have plenty of vacation time." I don't mention that the shop is downsizing and I've been putting applications in all around town just in case I get laid off. Plus, it's not like I don't have savings and I fully intend on working while I'm here. I just have to convince the stubborn blonde that she needs me.

"Oh, well in that case, you may regret the offer." She pats my leg. "You better go finish breakfast so we can eat. But hand me my crutches before you go?"

"You've got it, Mom." I hand them to her and head back to the kitchen. I really wish she didn't have to work anymore, and I'll do everything I can to ensure she doesn't have to.

* * *

After helping mom get settled, I get ready to head out. There are things I need to take care of. If it goes my way, any income I bring in will go straight to Mom. She's done everything in her power to take care of me. Now...it's my turn.

"I'll be back later." I bend down to kiss Mom on top of her head. "If you need anything, please call me. My phone will be in my pocket at all times."

She laughs, and I realize how much I've missed the sound. "Quit being a worry wart. I'll manage just fine."

"Okay, Mom. Just keep your phone nearby, please." Instead of sticking around to argue with her, I get my keys and walk out the door. The grocery store, and her list, will have to wait until after the first errand.

The roads are still wet, and I take my time driving to the bar. There's no use wrecking my car over roads that may be slick since I don't know the last time Asheville has had a decent rainfall. Lucky for me, the bar is less than ten minutes from home. I could walk here if I wanted to. The parking lot is half full when I pull in. It's good to know Out of the Ashes stays busy, even during the day. Angie's beat up car is parked front and center. You'd think after this level of success, she'd buy herself something new. At least, something dependable. I'm pretty sure that's the same thing she used to drive when she'd take me to football practices.

Putting my car in park next to hers. It looks out of place, but I don't care. This thing is my pride and joy. The one thing I was able to pour myself into after being cut from the football team and ostracized by my teammates. With my phone in my pocket, I get out of the car and lock it behind me. There's no telling how this is going to go. If anything, she may try to kick me out.

The same girl from yesterday is standing at the podium when I open the door. "How many?" She starts, but her jaw drops. "Hold on, you're the guy from last night, aren't you? The one that swooped in like a superhero and saved Angie from those assholes."

Huh, so I've already made a name for myself. "I don't know that I classify as a superhero, but yes. I'm Dylan." I hold my hand out to her.

"I would. I think that's the first time I've ever seen her need help." She places her hand in mine. "I'm Lisa."

"Nice to meet you," I shake, gently. Her hand is tiny in mine and I'm guessing she may even be younger than me. "Any idea where I can find our damsel?"

A glass slams on the bar before Lisa has a chance to respond. Both of us turn toward the noise. Angie is glaring at me, hand still on the glass. "If you ever call me a damsel again, I will knee you in the junk."

"Now, is that anyway to talk to the person you used to babysit? Or, the one that saved your ass last night?" I smirk and she throws the rag in her other hand toward me. It falls about halfway between us.

"I had it under control."

"You could have fooled me." Picking up the rag, I walk toward the bar. "I'm assuming there was no concussion since you're here today."

"Not that it's really any of your business, no. I don't have a concussion." She yanks the rag out of my hand and throws it somewhere beneath the bar. "Is there a reason you're here today?"

"Actually," I pull a seat out before sitting and resting my forearms on the bar top. "There is."

7

angie

NO. I shake my head in disbelief. This boy, I mean man, did *not* just waltz in here like he's someone and plop himself on one of my barstools. He must be out of his ever-loving mind if he thinks he can come in here and demand an audience with me. I mean seriously, who the hell does he think he is?

I pick up a new rag and continue wiping down the counters, waiting for him to say whatever he's come to say. I'm not trying to be hostile toward him, but I am trying to tamp down my attraction. It feels wrong to find someone I've known since they were a kid so damn hot. But here we are. Lisa is tilting her entire body toward us to see what chaos is undoubtedly about to go down. Soon, I'll have to check on the diners, but they can wait a bit.

"Aren't you going to ask me what it is I want?" He lays his forearms across the bar top and leans toward me. I don't miss the way his arms flex at the movement. He's definitely not the scrawny kid I used to babysit anymore.

"That depends." I pause in my cleaning. It's only lunchtime, but I know once the sun sets, more people will show up. It's inevitable. They keep this bar growing, though. We'll be able to double the capacity if Stella can talk me out of my fear of expanding this place. I really hope everything we've done has made Uncle Max proud.

"Depends on what?" I catch his smirk before I turn away, making sure the rest of the bar area is ready for this afternoon and evening.

"If it makes you leave faster." My back is to him so I can't see his reaction, but the laughter is mocking.

"Probably not. At least, if I get my way." Now I turn around. He's been in town less than a day, and he's acting like he can come in here making demands. I don't think so.

"Which is what, exactly?" My hands are on my hips and I feel like an adult waiting for their petulant child to tell them what they did wrong.

"Is that problem you had with those guys last night a common occurrence?" He pauses for a few seconds, but doesn't give me a chance to respond. "Because your bartender, Carlos, told me it's been getting worse."

That traitor. If he were here, I'd give him a piece of my mind. "I can handle idiots like those. I've spent my entire life in this bar. There's nothing that will knock me down."

Dylan leans back, crossing his arms over his chest. The t-shirt tightens and holy hell, he needs to stop doing that. "Really? Because you *did* get knocked down last night. This place has gotten a lot more traffic since I left. With that kind of growth, you need someone that can handle situations like those."

I shrug. He has a point, but I don't want to concede. "We've handled it just fine until this point. Is there a reason you're bringing this up?"

"Yep," he nods. "I want a job."

"Seriously?" He has to be kidding. Who knows how long he'll even be in town? I haven't seen him in years.

"Please, Angie." He slides off the barstool and walks around the bar until he's right in front of me. "I'll need something to do while I'm here helping my mom."

Great. "That means you'll end up leaving at some point in time. What am I supposed to do when that happens? As you can tell, we are short on staff as it is."

"I can help train someone to replace me when I know the date I'm leaving." He leans forward until we're mere inches apart. His light brown eyes hold so much of that boyish uncertainty from when he was young. "If it helps the decision-making process, I'm not keeping the money for myself."

What? If not for himself, then who? Maybe he has a girlfriend back home wherever that is. I'm already shaking my head no, when one of my lunch regulars calls my name. "I don't have time for this right now, Dylan. And I'm not sure what, I'd have you do, unless you have experience working in a bar."

Before he can respond, I walk to the end of the bar and head toward the dining area. I've got a job to do, and I don't have the luxury of hiring someone who's only going to leave in some unknown time frame. That's the problem I keep having. I'm trying to build something here, and besides Carlos and Lisa, I don't have anyone I can count on to help me do the work.

Mr. Jones is smiling as I approach his table. "What can I get for you?"

"A beer would be great," he grins.

"You know dang well, if I give you a beer your wife will

be up griping me out." I tap the top of the table, "how about some more sweet tea?"

"If you're going to be mean, that'll do, I suppose." I turn toward the bar, and he taps my arm. "Though what the wife doesn't know won't hurt her." He winks and laughs as I walk away. That man will be the death of either me or his wife. He tries to order a beer at least once a week.

The first time I served him one, his wife was up here the next day telling me under no circumstances am I to serve it to him again. His doctor was the one that said he couldn't have it, and she would love my support because she wasn't ready to lose him just yet. It was the sweetest thing I'd ever heard. Also, pretty amazing that their love has lasted all this time.

Most people see me as jaded or cynical, but I'm not. I can appreciate love; I just don't have time for it in my life. There hasn't been anyone here to pique my interest...until last night when Dylan Knight walked into my bar. Too bad I don't have time for whatever he might have to offer either.

The tea pitcher is at the end of the bar, and Dylan is standing next to it with a wide smile. "I can get tea for you. Or, anything else you need." Did he just look me up and down? That can't be right.

No, I shake my head. I'm not entertaining this idea. Not only will he be leaving at some unknown time, but he'll be a distraction. I don't need distractions. Not now. Not when Stella is working on taking the bar to the next level. "Thanks, but it's not that hard to make tea. Most of us have been doing it since we could reach the sink."

Without another word, I grab the tea and head back to Mr. Jones's table. "Here you go," I pour the tea in his glass. "You need anything else?"

"Nope," he shakes his head. "I'll need the check soon.

The wife has a honey-do list a mile long. I can only avoid it for so long before she comes looking for me."

"What does she have on it?" I think it's funny he acts like he doesn't want to do whatever she's come up with. He would move heaven and earth for that woman.

"She needs me to add mulch to her flower beds, and pull weeds."

"Well, you should have done that this morning. It's way too hot outside to do it now." I'll never understand why some people wait until the heat of the day to get anything done.

"No, ma'am. It means more lemonade and sweet tea breaks." Or maybe he's better at planning than I thought.

"I'll go grab your ticket and box up a little something for your wife."

"Thank you, Miss Angie." He's already digging his wallet out of his back pocket when I turn away from his table.

I don't bother stopping at the bar just yet for his bill. Dylan will no doubt be there asking me to give him a job. It's not avoidance. Well, not completely. I do need to get Mrs. Jones something to snack on. I slide through the kitchen doors and open the fridge. Patrick is grilling a burger and nods at my entrance. Yes, there are still a couple of slices of cheesecake leftover from last night. They are going to love this little treat. It's not much, but if I can do anything to bring them a bit of joy, I will.

"You weren't saving these for anyone, were you?" I ask Patrick.

"Nope," he flips a burger and hands me a container at the same time. I would have completely messed that up, but he pulls it off without a hitch. Honestly, I'm wondering why I didn't get him to train as a bartender. That may be something I talk to him about later.

With the cheesecake in the container, I close the lid and head out of the kitchen. I don't want to get in the way of all the cooking tidbits. We all know I have the potential to screw up his flow. My feet come to a halt as soon as the door closes. The audacity of this man.

Dylan is standing in front of the computer cashing out Mr. Jones. I *never* said he could work here, and he's taken it upon himself to do it anyway. "What are you doing?" My whisper is harsh and I hope like hell Mr. Jones can't hear me.

"Don't gripe at him," Mr. Jones says. So much for my whispering skills, I should work on that. "I was coming up here anyway. No use in you having to go back to the table just to come over here again." He slides his wallet back in his pocket. "I thought he worked here and had him take my payment."

Dylan looks over his shoulder at me and grins. "See, I was helping out. Just think how much more efficient this place will be with another staff member."

"He's right, Miss Angie." Mr. Jones nods. "After what happened here last night, you need a big young man like Mr. Knight to keep the fighting out."

"I don't ne—" My words die on my lips. "Wait. How do you know about what happened last night?"

"Everyone in town knows," he shakes his head. "I'll never understand these boys who think they have to fight to solve problems. I didn't want to ask about how you're feeling. If you're anything like my wife, you'd have my head."

Damn, the gossip got around town much faster than usual. I can't even imagine the wild stories going around about what actually happened. I can almost guarantee Mrs. Jones's friends are romanticizing Dylan's involvement. If they even knew it was him. I swear it feels like everyone in this town is eager for me to get into a relationship of some sort, except me.

"Probably," I smile, even though I want to hide behind my hands. "But, I'm fine. Nothing to worry about. I also banned them from the bar, so if they know what's good for them, they won't show up again." I hold out the container. "Now, here's something for you and your wife. Enjoy."

I'm trying to push him toward the front door, but he stopped before he's out. He looks me in the eye to make sure he has my full attention. "It would be a good idea to hire him, even if it's for something else. You can't run this entire place by yourself. I know there are a few other people, but you can't make this a success if you're trying to do it all."

"He's not staying, though. I'll have to find someone new when he goes home." And he's a distraction, dammit. I can't have him around here looking the way he does.

"Take the help while you can. Once you get some more employees it won't be so hard to let him go when he needs to." He gives me a one-armed hug, "Listen to an old man who's been through it before. You'll burn out and everything will fall. You've done a good thing with this bar. I'm proud of you."

"Thanks, Mr. Jones. That means a lot to me." I give him one final squeeze before slipping from his arm. "I'll consider it. It would be nice to give everyone more than one day off a week."

"Good," he nods. "Thanks for the goodies." He walks out the door, and I let his words mull over in my mind. He might actually know what he's talking about. Would it be so bad to have him here? Distraction or not, we desperately need the help.

I turn away from the door, looking for Dylan. He's standing at the end of the bar big, sad, puppy eyes hoping I say yes. Before I have a chance to offer him a job, an angry voice booms as the door opens. Great. I spin to see what the commotion is, and it's one of the assholes from last night. Another point proving that I need Dylan around, as much as I might not want it.

8

dylan

I COULD SEE it on her face. She was walking toward me, no doubt to tell me I could work for her. I kept the reasoning vague. If I told her, it was for my mom, she wouldn't have put me through the ringer. She would have done it because she's always had a soft spot for my mom. But no...the asshole from last night had to barge through the door. What part of banned do people not understand?

"I want to speak to the manager," he's yelling as soon as the door is open. "There was no reason for me to get kicked out last night."

Angie marches up to him, no doubt ready to kick him out again, but she stops just out of arms-length. A few of the diners get up from their tables and peek around the wall to see what is going on. Even more fuel to add to the rumor mill. I can bet some people who have always hated this place will use it as ammunition to get it shut down. "Sir, you're going to have to leave. I banned you from the bar indefinitely. If you can't abide by my rule, then I can, and will, call the police chief."

Go Angie. I always thought she was a badass when I was younger, but now I know she is. So, what if making money for my mom isn't the only reason I'm here? I can't deny seeing her last night after all these years piqued my interest. She doesn't look any older than the last time I saw her. The only difference is now I'm old enough to do something about it.

"I'm not leaving. Not until you tell me why I was kicked out when I didn't throw the first punch." Damn, he sounds like a toddler throwing a fit. He's slightly shorter than me, but he looks like he outweighs me. It won't be a problem if I have to step in again. I've played football most of my life, I'm used to taking down the big guys.

Angie lifts one hand and brushes a stray hair back into place. "Look, it doesn't matter *who* started the fight. The fact is, you were disturbing the atmosphere for the other patrons, and I will not have that happen in my bar." She crosses her arms and tilts her head. "Now, are you going to leave, or do I have to call the chief?"

He takes a step toward her, and I'm not taking any chances. What happened last night will not happen again. Not while I'm here. I rush to her side. "She asked you to go nicely." Stepping in front of Angie, I let the guy try to size me up. "If not, she will call the cops. But I can't promise I won't get you out of here myself before they arrive. And I can promise you, I won't be gentle."

Angie gasps behind me. It could be good or bad, I have no idea. The guy is glowering at me. He doesn't like being sized up and ridiculed in front of the patrons of the bar. He's slightly older than me and I don't know who he is. He has to be from one of the neighboring towns. If he was from Asheville, I would have recognized him.

He doesn't budge from in front of the door, and I can feel everyone's eyes on me, wondering what I'm going to do. I don't want to resort to fighting, but I will if it gets his ass out of here. Indecision crosses his face, and I take one step forward. Swinging distance. A hand lands on my forearm and I know it's Angie without having to look back. She doesn't want me to get physical. Sometimes, that's the only way to get the point across. People like this guy think they can do what they want with no regard, and I won't have it. Not when it comes to her, or the bar.

Finally, he seems to make up his mind. "This bar is trash anyway," he sneers. "There are better ones in Dallas." With those parting words, he slams the door open and stomps out. Good riddance.

Lisa claps from behind the host stand, and a few of the patrons join her. She turns toward Angie. "That was awesome. Can we keep him?" A few agreements are muttered from the dining area, and I can't help the chuckle escaping my mouth.

"He's not a puppy, Lisa." Angie wrinkles her nose. She looks up at me, and smiles. A real, honest, genuine smile. That's the moment I know I've won her over. At least, in this aspect. "But, yes, Dylan, you have a job here." I open my mouth to thank her, but she lifts a finger. "Not yet. Let me make sure everyone is okay, then we can talk about job responsibilities and all that in my office."

Not one to press my luck, I mime zipping my mouth shut and throwing away the key. Hopefully, I can keep my cool when it's just me and her. It'll be difficult not letting my crush on her all those years ago get in the way, but I'm determined.

* * *

Lisa is a delight as I wait for Angie to finish up with her customers. I'm not going to press my luck any further than I have with pestering her. She'll come get as soon as she's ready. Everyone went back to their table as soon as they saw there would be no actual drama. I swear, that's the one thing that annoys me about this town. They all need something to talk about that doesn't even involve them. There would be less fighting if people would mind their own business.

"You'll love working here." Lisa claps, excited about having another person to share the responsibilities. There's no doubt it'll take some of the stress and pressure off Angie, but also the people that work for her. "We are like family."

I don't want to burst her bubble, but even found families can turn their backs on you and make you feel like you don't fit in. Not that I know from experience or anything. Hell, it's pretty much the reason I left this place. I got tired of being the extra in our group. Even though Jake is really the only one that had a consistent girlfriend, there was Randall and Marshall. It's still an even number. There wasn't space for me most of the time. It could have also been my immaturity with being able to handle it, but I won't admit to that, ever.

"I'm sure it'll be great." I smile. "The biggest plus side is I know almost everyone since I went to school with them. But...you look around my age, and I don't remember you." It's not a dig. At least, I don't intend for it to be. I want to get to know my coworkers. Though I think Carlos has already made his mind up about me. We'll see when he comes in if I'm still here. There are a few things I need to wrap up before I actually start this new job.

Her cheeks turn pink, and she looks away. "I'm not from around here. This just happened to be a pit stop on my journey, and I decided to stay. Angie was kind enough to give me a job."

It's not often someone comes across Asheville and wants to stay. It's exactly what she said, a pit stop onto bigger and better things. Nobody comes here and chooses to put down roots. This girl is admirable for doing something so adventurous without a backup plan, and with nobody to have her back. Maybe we're more alike than I thought. I essentially did the same thing when I went back to school and stayed there. The only difference is I once upon a time had my teammates to help me out until all that went down the drain.

I shake my head and snap out of my thoughts, forgetting for a moment I'm having a conversation with someone. "She's pretty great like that. Always doing what she can to help others." Except me. I wonder what that's all about. Lisa could know the answer to that. "I don't want to overstep but, do you know why she was so resistant to me working here?"

Lisa chews on her bottom lip, and looks everywhere except at me. Yep, she definitely knows something. "Um, she hasn't mentioned anything to me." She's lying. "But I'm glad she changed her mind. We could really use an extra pair of hands around here. Well, we need about ten more pairs, if I'm being honest."

A shadow falls over me. I know who it is, but I want to make her squirm a bit. I wonder how much of the conversation she overheard. "So, what are you two talking about?" Is it just me, or did her voice go a notch higher at the end?

Lisa straightens and runs her hands over her shirt. "Not much, just letting him know how I stoked I am about another person working here. We'll have a full slate as soon as Stella puts on the job fair."

Stella? I've never heard that name before. Is she new in town? Another transplant on their way to somewhere else, but got stuck here? "Who is that?" I turn toward the petite blonde and wait for her to answer.

Angie smirks and crosses her arms over her chest. I won't say that it doesn't draw my attention to breasts. Her shirt is tight and low cut, and my eyes linger for a few seconds before I lift them to her face. Her cheeks blush, knowing exactly where I was focusing. She clears her throat. "She actually married Johnny not too long ago. You remember him, right?" I nod and she continues. "She's the one who helped me take it from biker bar chic to this. There are also a few more enhancements we're making soon."

"What else do you plan on doing?" This place can barely hold the crowd it brings in now. At least, that's the vibe I caught during my visit last night.

"You'll have to wait for the staff meeting." She turns toward the other side of the bar and starts walking. "Come to my office and we can discuss your job duties."

I don't hesitate. My ass is out of the stool and right behind her before she finished her command. I have the added bonus of watching her walk, and the view is so much better now than when I was a kid. Now...I can appreciate the woman she has become. As a teen, I had no idea.

Her office is at the end of the hallway, and I close the door behind me. Angie sits in a chair behind an old beat-up desk. I can only assume it was her uncle's and she refuses to part ways with it. Not that I blame her. From the little I remember; they were very close. "So, what all do you need me to do around here? I mean, other than throwing out the assholes that start bar fights."

"First," she holds up a finger. "We're not going to call them assholes outside of the office. Second, I won't really need you during the day, unless someone needs a day off to take care of things."

"That's fine with me," I shrug my shoulders. "I need to be around when mom is awake to help her out. Nights work a lot better anyway."

"Good." She opens a drawer and pulls a form out of her desk. "I need you to fill this out. Other than that, you'll be bussing tables and taking food to tables. I'd have you work bar, but I doubt you're certified."

"Nope." Leaning forward I rest my elbows on my knees. "I've never had a reason to, and if I was, I don't think it'd even be valid here since I live out of state."

"You're right," she nods. "Do you have any other experience working in a bar, or serving food? I want to make sure the transition is as easy as possible, at least while you're here. I also want at least two weeks-notice of when you're going to leave. I'll need time to replace you."

Wow, she's going hard with the questions. "I'm not an asshole employee. As soon as I know when I'm going back home, you'll be the first to know. Well, second, Mom would be the first." Now to address the rest of her concerns. "I bussed tables in college, so that part should be easy. As long as you teach me the layout of the tables, I can do what needs to be done to get the food out. I can even help out in the kitchen if you need me to. I'm a quick learner."

"I hope so." Angie sighs and leans back in her chair. "Why do you even want a job here? Especially when you aren't staying?"

"My mom." I grab the form off her desk and stand. "I

don't want her to keep working two jobs. She's getting older, and if I can make that easier for her, I will." I walk toward the door. "Give me any hours you want to throw at me, and I'll be here." Lifting the form in the air, I wave it around. "I'll have this filled out and brought back today. I need to get some groceries because Mom's fridge is empty."

"Look forward to it."

I'm not sure what to make of that. I open the door and head to the front of the bar. Hopefully, I can keep my whatever feelings these are toward her at bay. I'm not here for long, and I don't want her thinking I wanted the job because I used to crush on her. Even if that is a small part of the reason.

9

angie

HE WASN'T LYING when he said he'd have the employment form turned in the same day. We really could have used him last night, but I didn't want to spend the time training him on one of our busiest nights. The weekends here are brutal for those of us that have been here for the beginning. I can't imagine throwing him to the wolves right off the bat.

"Hey Ang," Lisa enters the bar and throws her purse on the nearest table. "Are we going to talk about the expansion during this morning's meeting?"

"Yep," I nod. "Everyone else should be on their way. I started the coffee pot a few minutes ago, and there are donuts on the table over there."

She claps her hands and bounces up and down. This girl is way too perky in the mornings. I'll have a dose of whatever she's having. "I'm starving." She rushes to the table with the donuts and grabs one before glancing over at me.

"So," she sing songs. "How do you think Dylan is going to work out?"

"We'll see, I guess." I shrug. "Hand me one of those, please?"

"Chocolate or glazed?"

"Definitely the chocolate." She grabs one and brings it over before sitting down in the chair next to me. "It only sucks that he won't be permanent. It's hard keeping people for a long period of time."

"At least you'll be able to ogle him anytime you want." She raises her eyebrows. "You can't tell me that wasn't a part of the reason you hired him."

Rolling my eyes, I take a bite of the donut. "That was the reason I *didn't* want to hire him. It feels weird to have any sort of reaction to the kid I used to babysit."

"Except he's not a kid anymore." She takes a bite of hers. "The way I see it both of you are adults. If he still has any kind of crush on you from his childhood days, I don't see how it's a bad idea to act on it." I open my mouth to argue, but she holds up a finger. "Look, I'm not going to be like Stella and try to hook you up with the perfect man. Every attempt she's made has failed. But, it's not wrong to hook up with a guy you clearly have a strong reaction to. I vote you have fun while he's here."

Leave it to Lisa to talk me into doing something with my attraction to him. "That would be an HR nightmare if things went south."

"You act like we have a HR department. Like I said, two consenting adults."

"Please tell me you're not thinking about banging the new guy." Carlos's voice scares the hell out of me. My knee hits the bottom of the table and I wince.

"Jesus, could you say that any louder?" He is nothing if

not straight to the point. That's one of the reasons I hired him all those years ago. He has zero problems dealing with drunk customers.

"Calm down," he sits on the other side of me. "Him and Stella were both pulling into the parking lot when I opened the door. They didn't hear anything." Thank God. I don't even want to think of what Stella would say. She'd make it this huge thing and try to force us into a relationship. Who's to say either of us even want the fun thing on the side. And if Dylan had heard, I'd be mortified. What thirty something year old gets all gooey like a hormonal teen at the sight of a good-looking man? Me, apparently.

Not two seconds later, Stella walks in with Dylan on her heels. "I see we have a new member of the family," she waves her hand in his direction. "Normally, we'd do the whole long introduction thing, but we've got a lot go over this morning."

Both her and Dylan grab chairs and sit down between Carlos and Lisa. "I'm all for being a close-knit group, but maybe we should move to a bigger table so we have some room."

"Good idea, Ang," Stella snaps her fingers and points toward the table Dylan and his friends occupied Friday night. "While y'all get settled, I'm going to grab a cup of coffee. Anyone else need one?"

We all shake our heads and she disappears around the corner. The rest of us stand and move toward the new table. Dylan sits down next to me. "So that's Stella? She seems like she runs a tight ship."

"She does, but I'm not mad about it. She's managed to help me make this the best bar in the county." With the way things are going, it could be one of the best in North Texas. But I'll be happy with continued success. As long as this place is a fun, and safe, place for people to let loose, I've done my job.

Stella comes back with a mug in her hand, grabs her bag and pulls out her phone. I don't think I've ever seen her without it. Her entire life is in that thing. "Okay, so first up on the list is the job fair. We're going to hold it here, of course. But we need to pick a morning during the week when we can shut the dining area down."

Dylan raises his hand as if he's in a classroom. "Wouldn't it be a good idea if we still allow customers to come in? We can section off an area for applicants, but they will get a chance to see the place in action. It's nice knowing what you're getting yourself into."

"Oh, that's a great idea," Stella says animatedly, making a few notes in her phone. "Thanks..."

"Dylan," he supplies and I can hear the pride in the way he says his name. It's good to know some things haven't changed. That was one of the things I always admired about him, even when he was a kid. He could have been cocky like Jake, but he wasn't. He took pride in everything he did. I'm assuming by his tone of voice, he still does.

"How do we feel about holding it this week, and then another next?" Stella is scrolling through what I can only assume is her calendar. "That will give more people a chance to come up and apply."

Lisa perks up. "Can we please? I love working here and all, but a day off would be great." She taps her finger against the table. "Actually, I might have someone that can also work the host stand. She won't need much training, and will be a great addition to the team."

"Sounds good," I nod. "I'm all for people who don't need a lot of hand holding." I glance at Dylan, wondering how much of a pain it's going to be to get him up to speed.

"Alright," Stella taps her phone a few more times. "I'll get with Angie and we'll pick a few days." Her eyes meet mine. "Now, she has an announcement, and we'll talk after she makes it."

Great, there goes hoping she would handle it for me since *she's* the one who talked me into it. I stand up and point toward the back wall. "I'm not sure if any of you have heard yet, but I bought the space next door to ours. It's been vacant for almost a year, and Stella and I decided it would be a good investment."

Carlos rolls his eyes, but waits for one of us to keep going. He's known about it because he saw the paperwork on my desk. To my surprise it's Dylan who speaks up before Lisa. "What are you going to do with it?"

"Well," Stella clears her throat. "The plan is to open up part of that wall and make the bar bigger. We're already almost at capacity and the extra room means more customers." She pauses for dramatic effect, and I wish she'd just spit it out already. "But...we're also going to add live music."

"Is that why we have a sudden push for more employees?" Lisa asks. "I've noticed workers going in and out of there, but I assumed someone else had bought it. I didn't know you did." She nods her head toward me.

"Part of the reason, but also because we desperately need the help. I'm wanting to grow our team, and have reliable people here. Uncle Max told me to make this place the best it can be, and after a lot of persuading, Stella talked me into it."

"What will that mean for us and the way we work now?" Now Carlos has questions.

Stella is the one to take the lead this time. "Honestly, not much. We'll have to shut down for a couple of days when they demo the wall and get it framed, but other than that, we'll have more people to share the workload."

"And what kind of music will you have?" Dylan turns to face the wall, trying to picture it. "Will it be local artists, or are you going to open it up to bigger names? Both will come with their own growing pains."

That's a good question, and one I've thought about since Stella brought it up to me. "I want to focus on local talent. It'll give them some place safe to play and be heard. The only exception is the weekend we open it up."

"Oooo," Lisa is intrigued. "Who will be playing for that?"

I prepare myself for the excitement she's about to display. "Crooked Halo." I was right, Lisa jumps out of her chair and claps her hands like a cheerleader at a football game.

"Seriously," Dylan's eyes widen. "You know those guys?"

Huh, it feels good knowing I can shock him. At least it's some sort of reaction from him toward me. Though, I'm almost certain he would have gone all caveman the other night if Tonya hadn't offered to take me to the emergency room. Hell, I thought he was going to demand he take me himself for a second. So maybe his teenage crush on me is over, and he outgrew it. He gave up pretty easily. That's something I never thought he'd do.

"Sort of," I shrug. "It's more of Stella's doing than mine. Her cousin's fiancé does all their merch and handles their website."

"That is pretty awesome." He nods appreciatively. "You know that's going to draw in a huge crowd. Even if I'm back home by then, I'll come down and help you out with crowd control. You're going to need full-time muscle once the live music becomes a regular thing."

He has a point. I never planned on hiring a bouncer for it because I've always handled things on my own. Well, until the other night. That was a mistake on my part. I still have a knot on my head from where I hit the floor. It takes everything in me not to rub it and show any sort of weakness. "We'll cross that bridge when we get there."

"You need to cross it now," Carlos mutters. I don't miss the way he's side-eying Dylan. He doesn't trust him. He also doesn't *know* him.

"What was that?" He knows I heard him, but if he has comments, everyone in the room needs to hear them.

"I said," he crosses his arms over his chest. "You need to cross that bridge now, at the job fairs. If we're going to need any sort of security for future crowd control, we need to already have them on the staff learning the ropes. Especially since he won't be here forever." He points his finger in Dylan's direction. "And the crowd has gotten rowdier in the past few months."

"Do you have a problem with me?" Dylan doesn't stand or move a muscle, but the threat is evident in the clench of his jaw.

"I don't know you, but I do know that you're going to work here and then leave us high and dry."

"I'll train whoever I need to in order to keep this place safe. I didn't see anyone else running to help when Ang got between those two assholes."

"Boys," I slam my hand on the table. "You are both grown adults. Right now, you're acting like kids having a pissing contest. I need both of you to get along if we're going to make this a success." I point my finger at Carlos. "Dylan is an old friend. I trust him to do his job, and whatever else I throw at him."

Carlos mutters something else, but I don't catch what it

is. Dylan smirks and I have a feeling I don't want to know what he said.

Stella's eyes are bouncing between all of us, wondering what she's missed. Hopefully she doesn't see the tension I have around Dylan. I won't lie, him choosing the chair next to me sent butterflies tumbling through me. But she doesn't need to know that. She'll be in matchmaker heaven and I'm not ready to deal with that. "Okay," she says softly. "I'll get the job fair ready to go, and y'all can do whatever it is you do until you open up later."

Carlos stands and heads to the door, Lisa right behind him. Stella grabs her bag and goes to my office, leaving me and Dylan alone. Shit.

10

dylan

FINALLY, alone with her. I don't know what that dude's problem is, but he needs to get over it. As much as I don't like the way he *didn't* handle the situation Friday night, the attitudes we have toward each other will only stress out Angie. I do, however, wonder if she heard what he muttered under his breath. The comment about me being her eye candy is all I needed to hear. It's good to know she realizes I exist now. And not in some poor kid she used to take care of way.

I stay glued to my chair, waiting to see if she gets up. She doesn't. "So, what was all that about? He met me for a whole five minutes and already has me pegged." He's not the first person to do it, and I'm sure he won't be the last. I've dealt with guys like him my entire life. From coaches to teammates that didn't have to use scholarships to get into college. To them, I'm just some pity case from the wrong side of the tracks.

Angie waves the question away. "Ignore him, He's over-protective of me and Lisa."

"What about Stella?"

She laughs. "He doesn't have to be. If anything, ever happened while she was here, Johnny would be here in two point five seconds, ready to kick someone's ass."

That sounds about right. Johnny has always been the protector type. Him and his grandpa were nice enough to let us party in the pasture when we were in high school. As long as we didn't make a mess, or destroy anything, we could go out there whenever we wanted. Some of my best, and worst, memories are in that empty field.

"I believe it." I turn in my chair, and it's just enough for my knees to touch hers. I don't miss the slight shiver that passes through her at my touch. I shouldn't still be attracted to her after all these years. Especially not now. Not when I'm going to be leaving as soon as my mom is able to get around on her own again. "Is he still the same way with you? I know y'all were like siblings."

"Pretty much." For a split second, it looks like she's going to move, but she doesn't. She relaxes her body and her knee slides further up my leg. Damn it, working here might be a mistake. How am I supposed to keep her off limits when all I want to do is grab her and have my way with her? "He wasn't happy when I took over the bar and let go of the manager my uncle had working for him. I mean, you remember the crowd that used to come in here, right?"

Yeah, it was where all the local bikers came to hang out. They weren't bad people, but when some of them drank too much, it could get a little worrisome. Not that I would know from experience. Angie worked here in her downtime and would shoo me away anytime I came near the place. "It wasn't all bad. If anything, I'm sure they had respect for you. When you weren't carting me around, you were here, helping out your uncle."

"I'm sure most of them did. But there were those few that couldn't hold their liquor and temper." She sighs. I'm not sure if it's because she misses those days. When her uncle was still here and taking care of this place. Or, if it's because she doesn't think she can manage all the changes coming at her. I know it's been a while since he passed, but from what I can tell, he'd be damn proud of her.

I lean forward to offer her some comfort but Stella's voice stops me in my tracks. Okay, most of it was for comfort, but a part of me just wants to hold her. Feel her in my arms the way I could only imagine as a scrawny sixteen-year old. "Angie, are you ready to go over the calendar? I want to get some fliers made up and make an announce-ment in the paper as soon as I can."

Angie leans back and sighs. "Yeah, let's get this thing going. We need all the help we can get at this point." She scoots out her chair and stands. Placing a hand on my should, she gives me a quick pat. "I know last night I said I mostly needed you in the evenings, but do you think you could come back when we open up at lunch? We also close early on Sundays, so it wouldn't be a full day."

I'll take whatever time I can get. Earn money and spend time with the girl I spent so many years fantasizing over, it's a win all the way around. "Sure thing. Just let me know what time. Can we also figure out what my schedule will be so I can let Mom know the nights I'll be home late?"

Damn, I sound just like that teenage boy all over again. Having to check in with mom before I do anything. It's not for her to keep tabs on me, though. It's respect since I'm living with her until she's better. Or, at least mobile without help.

Angie shocks me when she smiles. "Absolutely. I bet she isn't used to you being home and coming in at hours she doesn't set for you." Like she ever set in hours. She would always crash before I came home. Exhausted from working two jobs.

"I just like to let her know. She worries."

"I get that. My mom still makes me check in with her so she knows nothing happens to me." She laughs and shakes her head. "Parents just never stop thinking about their kid's safety."

"You've got that right." I stand and lean in for a quick hug. I don't know why I do it. It's instinct, thanks to my upbringing with my mom. "What time do I need to be back?"

She slides out of my hold. "Oh, right. Noon? We usually open at one, but it'll give me a chance to help you learn the tables and show you around the place before we have customers."

"I'll see you then." She turns toward the hallway to her office. I should go now, but I love watching her walk away. The way her jeans hug her figure is perfection.

* * *

It's eleven thirty when I get back to the bar. I stopped at Brews Clues on the way. If there's anything I remember, it's that Angie is a workaholic. Stella brewed her own cup this morning, but Angie is definitely worth the extra effort. Not only because of my crush, but also because she deserves it. She helped take care of me when my mom needed her help, and the fact that she's given me this job to better Mom's life, she more than deserves it.

The entire bar is empty when I open the door. Where is everyone? I know Angie said noon, but I didn't think I would be the first to arrive. It's par for the course with me. Even back home, I'm one of the first to arrive at the shop and last to leave. Who knows? It's probably something Mom instilled in me since she's always been such a hard worker. Always picking up the slack and trying to prove her worth. No matter how much older I get, the same sort of pressure settles on me. Always trying to prove myself valuable. For my employer? Sure. But always that I'm worthy for my friends and family. It's a never-ending battle when you're always left out.

Grunts from the back of the building pull me out of my thoughts. "Angie," I call out. I don't get a response, even though I know it has to be her. The only car int he parking lot belongs to her.

Setting the coffee cups on the bar, I head down the hallway. My boots hitting hard on the floor. Scaring her isn't something I want to do. I remember being a kid and watching her go at it with her brother. She can hold her own, and I don't want to be on the receiving end if she gets freaked out. Not to mention how many people twice her size she's most likely stood up to. I'm choosing to protect my face.

Even with all the noise I'm making, she still must not hear me. There's scuffling sounds coming from the office and I open the door. Angie is on her tiptoes. Her hands above her head, holding on to the sides of a box. This isn't going to end well. I'm shocked she doesn't have a step stool or ladder. Or get someone who works here and won't fall backward to get it down for her. Another grunt as she tries to get a better grasp on the box.

"Here," I say from behind her. "Let me give you a hand."

She jumps and turns toward me. The box, already hanging off the shelf, falls forward and I pull her toward me. Hands waving in the air, trying to catch her balance, she stumbles and we hit the ground at the same time the box does. Me, on my back, and her on top of me. This isn't exactly what I pictured when I said I wanted to hold her in my arms.

Angie leans up, and pushes her hair aside, trying to get it out of her face. Her elbow jabbing into my ribs. At the sound of my grunt, she rolls off me. Those two seconds of contact may be the best ones I've had in a long time. I'm no saint, but nobody could ever compare to her. The girl I've always wanted but could never have. Until now. Even though I'm not staying doesn't mean I can't make my move.

"What the hell are you doing here?" She shrieks and stands. Feeling the need to put herself in a powerful position. I don't know why. She's one of the strongest women I know. I get it though; she needs to make herself feel like she can cut it in an industry run mostly by men. She's not so different from me trying to prove myself to anyone, and everyone, that shows me an ounce of attention.

"I, uh, came in early." I look around the space to see what fell from the box. Hopefully, it wasn't anything breakable. Fabric covers the floor and the box is busted. "I heard sounds back here and wanted to make sure you were okay."

"Oh," she straightens her shirt, covering the sliver of skin on display. "I didn't hear you." Her cheeks look pink. Is she blushing? "My ear buds were in and I wasn't expecting anyone just yet. Everyone else gets here right at twelve." She holds the ear buds that fell out when we went tumbling as proof.

"Obviously," I laugh. Standing up, I dust off my pants. They aren't really dirty, but I need to do something before I make an ass out of myself. You know, like put my arms around her, or something equally ridiculous. "I also brought you coffee." Another glance at the pile of fabric on the floor. "Do you need help with anything?"

"No, I've got it." She bends down to pick up the pile and places it on her desk. She kicks the box to the side on her way around to sit down. "I had to pull down the aprons to get one for you and anyone else we hire from the job fair. I forgot I put it at the top."

Clearly. I want to be a smart ass, but I know it'll get me nowhere. "Do you need me to put them back up? Or are we going to leave them down?"

"You know you don't have to help yet. You still have," she glances at her computer. "Ten more minutes before you're even supposed to be here."

"I like getting to work early. It gives me a chance to get in my work zone. And, like I said, I brought coffee." I point toward the hallway. "It's sitting on the bar."

She laughs, and even if she is stressed, I can't help but hear the pure joy in it. "Not much has changed with you, has it?"

"What do you mean?" The question isn't meant to be offensive, but I can't help thinking she's making a dig. Everyone else does.

"You like preparing, that's all. When you were a kid, you used to ask me to get you to practice thirty minutes early so you could get in the zone. Therefore, you haven't changed." She leans back in her chair. Her gaze travels up and down my body.

"That's true," I nod. "But there are so many other ways in which I have." This is my chance to let her know how I felt back then and how I think I still might. It's worth a shot, right? "I mean, surely, you've noticed. If the way you're looking at me is any sign."

Her eyes snap to mine. Good, I caught her off guard. Something I've never managed to do. "I don't know what you're talking about." She stands so fast her chair nearly topples over. "We should, uh, get up front. Everyone else will be here soon and we need to get you started on your training."

For someone who has zero issue running into fights she has no business interfering with, she sure is great at avoiding questions. "Yeah," I grin. "But when you're ready to admit that you've been checking me out when you think no one is looking, let me know." With a wink, I turn and walk out of the office. I laid the groundwork, and now I only have to wait. Fingers crossed it works in my favor.

11

angie

TWO WEEKS. Two freaking weeks since Dylan practically admitted he still has a thing for me. I mean, I knew he did when he was a teen. Hell, he tried asking me on a date the day he turned eighteen. I felt awful when I turned him down. It was like I stole his toy or kicked his puppy. I felt awful for letting him down. In my eyes, he was still just a kid.

I saw him one other time. The first summer after he went away from college. But he never approached me. I thought his crush was over. It was a done deal. But now, he's not some kid I looked after once upon a time. He's one hundred percent a grown man. And...he called me out on my bullshit. As much as I tried to hide it, Dylan saw every single one of my quick glances. Every look I shot his way. That must have been the ego boost he needed to confront me. Can I blame him, though? It's not like I was giving him clear signals.

"Ang?" Lisa knocks on the office door before stepping

inside, pulling me out of my head. "Are you ready for the new hires? They are standing around like a bump on a log with zero direction."

"Huh?" Focus. That's what I need right now. I have people that actually want a job, and going off the rails over Dylan is only going to get in the way. No matter how attracted I am to him.

"The new hires? We need to go over this orientation thing Stella set up." She squints her eyes at me. "Are you okay?"

"Yeah, I'm fine." I stand tall from my chair, trying to give off the bravado I don't feel.

"Are you sure? You've been acting really weird lately." She puts her hands on her hips and the stance reminds me so much of my mom, who I've also been avoiding. "Does it have something to do with Dylan?"

"Nope. I'm one hundred percent fine." Walking around the desk, I loop my arm through hers. "Just stressed with so many more new employees."

"You shouldn't be," she bumps into me. "More workers means more shared work. Which also means we can have actual days off." Her voice rises with the last statement. It sends a pang through my body. Don't get me wrong, it's something to be excited about, but it means I've been over-working her, Carlos, and Patrick. I never wanted that to be the case for them.

"You've got that right." I do my best to keep my tone cheerful. Lisa is very empathetic and I don't want her worrying about me when she doesn't need to. It's not her job to worry. It's mine, as the owner.

The new hires are no longer standing around when Lisa and I turn the corner. The new bartenders are at the bar with Carlos, and Dylan has a group in the dining area. Look at these two taking charge of the situation. If Carlos doesn't watch it, I'll end up promoting him to assistant manager. Then he can stress right along with me.

Lisa opens her mouth to speak, but I shake my head. "We can do the orientation part afterward. It looks like the guys have everything under control." Lisa shrugs her shoulders and heads back to the host stand. She rifles through a couple of papers. It's probably the application for her position. She wanted final say over who would be working up there, and I gave it to her. She's an important part of my team and she needs to know I take her seriously.

Leaning against the wall, I take in the surrounding sight. Even when my uncle had this place full, there were never enough employees to carry the burden. And, as of right now, we can rotate it so that we each get a break.

My focus is all on Dylan, though. He's a quick learner, I'll give him that. He's showing the waitstaff and bussers the table numbers. Taking them to each table, and quizzing them on the location. It's something they'll need to know during the lunch time rush and when the tables fill up at happy hour. He's good with them, and I want to ask him what his job normally is. There's a certain patience he has that I don't think I've ever been able to pull off well.

He must feel my gaze on him because he looks back. Surprise flashes across his eyes for a second before a wide smile takes over. He enjoys that I watch him. Knowing I have a pull toward him, but refuse to do anything about it. I can't.

It would be frowned upon for so many reasons. One, I'm his boss. That's already a huge no-no. Two, I used to babysit him. It might not matter to us, but this is a small town and people will talk shit. And three, probably the most important reason, he's not staying. Why would I set myself up for that disappointment? We could do a no strings attached sort of thing, but really how often does that actually work? Look at Johnny and Stella, they were trying to do that and they are now happily married. That type of heartache is not my cards. Not when I already have so much on my plate.

"A penny for your thoughts," Carlos comes to stand beside me.

"Believe me, you don't want them." I shake loose any thoughts I might have about telling Dylan I want him as more than just an employee.

"Yeah, you're probably right," he points toward Dylan, "especially if they have to do with him."

"What is your beef with him, anyway? You barely know him."

"He seems like the cocky type. The type who takes what he wants without thinking of the repercussions." He's not wrong. At least the first assessment. Dylan has always known he was good at football. It's what sent him to college. But he has always been a thinker. The silent friend that won't react without knowing the outcome. Something Jake needed when he was growing up.

"Just give him a chance, Carlos," I nudge him with my shoulder, "I think you'll find you're more alike than you think."

"Please don't say that," he grimaces, "I love you, and would do anything for you, but I do *not* want you looking at me the way you look at him."

"I don't know what you're talking about."

"Okay," he scoffs. "You might not know, but anyone in the same room as you two can sense it. It's honestly kind of annoying."

"Geez, thanks for the pick me up."

"Just keepin' it real." He laughs and heads back to the bar where the group he was leading is learning the bar layout. He's right about one thing, if I don't want people talking, I need to keep my eyes off Dylan.

* * *

"Ang, can you grab another case of straws? We're almost out of them." Carlos calls from behind the bar. I would say this is a new employee job, but they would spend way too long looking for it. The storage room, also my office, may be tiny, with shelves and boxes all over the place, but I know where everything is.

"Sure thing," I touch the screen of the computer a few more times. "Let me get this ticket settled up and I'll get it for you."

As much as having new people will be amazing, there's a part of me that worries they'll leave like everyone else before them. Maybe it's me? I could be a shitty boss and not even realize it. Why else would employees leave at the rate they do? My fingers are crossed this time I've found the right people. Stella and I meticulously went through the applications, picking those that we thought would hold some longevity.

With the ticket done, I pull the receipt off the printer and rush it over to the table. If Carlos says they're running low on something, it's usually because it's almost out. We're pretty busy for a Sunday afternoon, and I'm glad for the help we have. I motion toward Kim, one of the new hires and point over my shoulder. "Can you watch the tables while I grab some supplies for Carlos?"

"Yep," she smiles and "I've got you covered."

The hallway to the office is a short distance away, and I

make my way toward it. The loudness of the bar fades away the closer I get to the office. Now where is that box? Scanning the shelf, I don't see it anywhere. I squeeze behind the door, bumping it slightly as I reach up to look at the boxes higher on the shelf. There. Of course, it's on the top one. I really need to get some kind of a ladder in here. Especially since there are more people working here that may need to get something.

My hand goes up to grab the box, and I feel a sudden presence behind me. The door creaking before a soft thud as it shuts. "Here, let me help you with that."

Before I have a chance to turn around or offer any sort or rebuttal, Dylan's hands are covering mine on the box. They are warm and softer than I expected, and I can't deny the sparks that course through my body at the contact. My hands slide off the box as he brings it down in front of us. Me, caught between him and the shelf. "You didn't have to do that. I'm perfectly capable of pulling a box down."

I turn around to face him. That was a mistake. With my back to him, I could pretend his mere presence didn't have an effect on me, but now...I don't know if I can hide my reactions as easily. "You sure about that? The last time you tried aprons fell all over the floor."

Don't look up. Don't look up. Keep your eyes focused in front of you. His chest is perfectly reasonable to talk to, right? "And that's because you intervened." Jesus, this is ridiculous. My eyes move up his body. Above his chest, to his chiseled jaw, and up until I can see his eyes. Yep, big mistake. They hide nothing. Want simmers in their deep brown depths. The ball is in my court, and the way he's looking at me makes it hard to keep my wits about it.

A part of me wants to knock the box out of his hands and climb him like a tree. The other part knows damn well I don't need to venture down this path. This way lies heartache and broken promises. "Angie, are you still with me?" The box holding the mini straws and napkins falls to the floor. "Hello?"

That shakes me out of my thoughts. "Yeah, sorry what were you saying?"

"I was talking smack on your awesome box getting skills." He bends down until he's eye level with me. "Are you okay?"

"Yeah, I'm fine. I just can't think." I turn, but I'm trapped between Dylan and the shelf. His arms are on either side of me. My hand goes to his arm to push him away and stop at the sound of his voice.

"Is there a reason you can't think? Am I that reason?" I don't have to see his face to know he's smirking. I can tell by his voice, low and seductive. When the fuck did he master that?

"Does it matter?" I try for annoyed, but it's clearly not working. "I need to get this box to Carlos."

"Okay," he leans in closer. His breath a soft whisper against my ear. "But, answer one question." He waits for me to speak up, and I don't. I want to know what he's going to ask. "Do you feel anything toward me? I think I've made my interest pretty damn clear."

I could lie. Lying would be a hell of a lot easier, but I can't. Not now. Not with him so close to me. "I'm attracted to you. In ways I shouldn't be." A glance toward him is all it takes to know that he doesn't give a damn that I shouldn't have any feelings toward him. A wide grin is all I can see. And fuck if I don't want to kiss him. To see if he's as confident as he lets on.

My toes lift of their own volition, and I do just that. I need to know. Maybe then whatever the hell I'm experiencing around him will stop. I mean for it to be a quick peck, but soon my lips are parting and I'm deepening the kiss. I fully expect him to pull away, or grab me. Something to give me an idea of what he's thinking. All I can hear is the metal shelf behind me shaking. He has some restraint at least.

Before I can pull away the door opens and we jump apart from each other. "Angie, did you find the straws and napkins?" Carlos asks as he rounds the door. Dylan picks up the box and hands it to him before hurrying out of the office. Carlos pins me with a glare. "I sure hope you know what you're doing, Ang."

12

dylan

DAMN IT. I was so close. So fucking close to pulling her into my arms. She finally admitted to being attracted to me. But Carlos has to come in at the most inopportune moment and screw it up. I don't know that I'll ever forget the taste of her lips. The sweet Chapstick as she pressed her mouth to mine. It took everything in me not to wind my fingers through her hair and deepen the kiss. My grip on the shelf likely left the wire bent. Every part of me that wanted to claim her as mine was put into that shelf. She needed to lead the way. To let me know what she was okay with. Now, I don't know if I'll ever get the chance again. Fucking Carlos.

My mind is going a mile a minute at what that kiss means, and I bump into someone on my way down the hall. "Woah, slow down Dylan." Lisa puts her hands on my chest to get my attention.

"Sorry, I didn't see you there." Running my fingers through my hair, I take stock of my surroundings. The new employees are doing their jobs, and everything seems to be running smoothly. What am I even saying, I'm just as new as these guys. It doesn't feel that way, though. Angie and everyone treated me like I've been here forever the day I started. Even Carlos has been less of a dick toward me, though that might change after today.

"Obviously," she scoffs. "You look like the hounds of hell are on your heels."

I glance back toward the office and shake my head. "Nope. No hellhounds. But I should probably get back to work."

Shifting my body to the right, I start to go around her but she blocks my path, a mischievous gleam in her eye. "Wait, did...did something happen with you and Angie?" She peeks around to see if anyone close by is listening. "If so, it's about damn time. You two have been tiptoeing around each other and it was bound to happen."

Of course, she would be the one to notice, though I don't see how anyone else hasn't. I haven't exactly made my own desires secret. Maybe I should have until she figured her own shit out. "It's not really my place to say anything." That should deter her from any further questioning.

It doesn't. "Look, secrets aren't a big thing around here. We all pretty much know everything. Give me some sort of confirmation, at least. If you don't, I'll just bug the hell out of her until she relents."

She's a like a dog with a bone. Never giving up until she gets what she wants. "Fine," I groan. "Something might have happened, but I don't know where it's going to go or what it means. Can you keep it on the down low until I have a chance to talk to her?"

"As long as you talk to her after we close, I can do that." She points toward the office. "By the way, is Carlos back there? One of the new bartenders is freaking out. I know we hired them to see if they could handle the job even though they are brand new to bartending, but if she keeps on like this, I don't know how we're going to be able to keep her. She's not doing well with the fast pace."

That could potentially be a problem, but it's not mine. "Yeah, he's grabbing the box of supplies he needs."

"I see," Lisa smiles. "You get back out there. If anyone comes up to the stand while I'm back there, can you show them to a table?"

"You got it." I give her a thumbs up and exit the hallway. That must be what Tonya feels like when Cami gets a whiff of something changing. I honestly don't see how she handles it. I felt like I was under interrogation. I've never been on the receiving end of that. At least, not in a long time. I was the guy that went along with my group. Not in a bad way, but I never put up much fuss with change. It was something I was used to. Mom's work schedule shifted all the time, and I had to learn to work with it and accommodate her new hours.

Now I need to focus on the rest of my shift. The hard talk will come in a bit. My fingers and toes are crossed I'll get the reaction I want. I'm tired of waiting for her to see me. Angie was right about one thing; I typically go after what I want when it comes to sports and work. I'm nothing if not persistent. Now, it's time to do the same for my personal life.

* * *

The bar is finally quiet. Even though I've only been here two weeks, we were definitely busier today than any other that I've worked. It seems weird for a Sunday. Not so much the lunch time crowd, that we expect since folks are eating as a family after church or when they finally decide to roll out of bed. It was after that. We never got a lull in the crowd. It made for a rushed training experience with myself and the new people that started today. My only advantage is I've been here at nights when the place is crowded and on the verge of hitting fire code. It'll be nice when they open up the extra space. It'll give everyone a bit more room to move around.

"I think that's everything." One of the new girls yells from the other side of the room. The tables are cleaned off and the floors mopped. The work goes faster with more hands on deck.

Everyone makes their way to the computer to clock out and leave. Their families waiting for their arrival. It's my favorite part of working on Sundays. I get home at a decent time and can watch TV with Mom before she goes to bed. I didn't realize how much I missed spending time with her until I came back home. I guess that's because I saw so little of her when I was a kid. Her hours were all over the place to support me and my ambitions.

Carlos leaves with a wave over his shoulder, not once looking back to see if anyone is behind him. Lisa pauses at the stand, straightening everything up for tomorrow morning. When it's to her liking, she glances my way and gives me a thumbs up and mouths "good luck" before walking out the front door. It's just me and Angie.

I'm watching her as she makes sure she has everything. Cash in the deposit bag and a tally of the revenue for the day. She glances up and realizes I haven't left yet. "You don't have to stay. Everything has been done."

"I know," I grin and pull out a chair at the bar. "But I think we both know we need to talk after what happened earlier this afternoon." Bold? Maybe. I need to know, though. Plus, this is the only way I know of to keep us both in the same space without her running off or avoiding me. I mean, she could just leave, but I don't have any keys to lock up. Basically, she's screwed and has to stay. I feel slightly bad, like I'm taking advantage of the situation, but I need answers. This is the only way to make it happen.

"Do we have to?" She whines even though she's a grown ass woman. I know I should find it annoying, but it's adorable. This is probably the only time I've seen her actually face something that gives her pause.

"Yes. As much as I know you don't want to, we need to figure out whatever this is between us." She opens her mouth to argue, but I put my finger up to shush her. "I know you're going to say it's me playing out my childhood fantasies, but it's more than that."

"How do you know?" She sets her stuff down and pulls out a barstool three spots down to sit on. It's still not close enough to me, but I'll let her have this space...for now. "You've had a crush on me since you were ten, and it continued until you were in high school. How do you know this isn't some bang your babysitter fantasy you can finally play out?"

I think back to the day I turned eighteen. All the things I thought I did right. Flowers, check. Nice outfit, check. Well, as nice as one as I had at the time. It was still jeans and a button up with whatever shoes I had on after practice. I pulled up to her house in my beat-up cash car. It wasn't much, but it was something I worked hard that summer to pay for. It was mine and mine alone.

Her car was in front so I knew she was there. It was now or never. I grabbed the flowers and marched up her stairs like a man on a mission. She answered after a few knocks. I thought the surprise on her face was a good thing. I rushed through my words, "Angie, I'd like to take you out on a date." She was stunned silent, and it was the first time I'd ever seen her without a witty comeback. I did it. She was only taking a second to say yes. But...a man I didn't know came up behind her and started laughing.

I didn't bother sticking around. I hightailed it back to my car and sped off. That was the end of my pursuing anything serious. I don't know how long she dated that guy, but I hope like hell it wasn't long.

"Dylan?" Angie pulls me out of the past and the heartache I felt then.

"Sorry." I shake my head and glance toward the bar. "Maybe we need a drink for this."

Angie stands and makes her way around the bar. I think she's going to pull a couple of beers from the cooler, but no, she grabs two shot glasses and the bottle of whiskey. "I think that's a good idea."

When she sits there's only one barstool separating us. The thought of shots seems to have loosened her up a bit. It breaks down a wall where we can truly speak what's on our minds. She pours the liquid into both glasses and slides one in my direction. I down it and set it on the bar top. "Look, I know this is probably coming from left field for you, but I've always liked you. For the longest time, I thought my crush would fizzle and fade, but it hasn't. If anything, being here has only made it grow stronger. It's brought about what ifs and I would love to see where they go."

Angie doesn't say anything for a few minutes, only sips on her shot. I assume it's to gather her words. Maybe handle this situation more delicately than she did all those years ago. I'm not an insecure eighteen-year old boy anymore, though. I've grown up a lot since then. I had to after all the bullshit that happened with football and then get on my feet by myself without a support system. I'm capable of hearing whatever she has to say now. But she needs to understand that I'm not backing down without a fight. I can't. Not when I have the one person I've always wanted within my grasp.

"I don't understand what the point would be, Dylan. Have you changed your mind about sticking around?" Of course, that's the thing she focuses on. She waits for me to answer, to give her confirmation that I don't have.

"Being home hasn't been as complicated as it was when I was growing up, but I can't make any promises. I had a life before I came back to Asheville, and I'll have one to get back to when Mom is on the mend." It doesn't need to be mentioned that I might not have a job when I go home. I don't want to give her false hope.

"Then why would us seeing about what ifs be a good thing?" She pours us both another shot. "Say, we give this thing a shot. Everything is going great, and then bam it's time for you to leave. What do we do then? How can we have a successful relationship when you're hours away and I'm married to this place." Well, when she puts it like that it seems impossible. I won't let that deter me.

"That's a risk you'd have to be willing to take. All relationships are. You can't bank on them working or not working. I mean, you took the risk to make this bar into something I'm sure nobody in this town thought it would live up to." Let's be real, most of the people in this town hoped it wouldn't because in their opinion it's an eyesore on the wholesome place they want outsiders to believe it is. And at one time, it might have been. But not now, she's made this one of the best places to hang out. Whether it's the lunch time crowd, early dinner for families, or folks wanting to blow off steam after work. I don't get why she wouldn't take the same risk when it's for her.

"That's something I can measure in numbers and goals. I can't do that with a relationship. It's why I haven't had one in years. They don't understand how much time this place takes from me." This time she takes the whole shot and slams it on the counter. "And what happens when things don't work out with us? You still work here. That would make things a hell of a lot harder on everyone working here. What kind of precedent does that set?"

"Then we talk about it, and handle it, like the adults we are." It's really not that hard, I don't know why she's making it a whole thing.

She stands and puts the tequila up on the shelf where it belongs and sets our glasses in the sink. "Look Dylan, as much as I might want to see where we could go, I can't right now. I have too much on my plate with the renovations and opening up more space." She grabs her keys and the deposit bag. She slides a different set of keys toward me. "Lock up before you leave."

And then she's gone. Walking out the front door and away from what could be a good thing. I wasn't playing, I'm going to fight for this chance. Her words confirmed her feelings, and that's all I needed to hear.

13

angie

WHY DOES he have to do this? Now of all times. He knows how much stress I've been under. He's been privy to the same information Stella, Carlos, and Lisa have. It's part of the reason I slid my bar keys to him. I trust him with the bar. Too bad I don't trust anyone with my heart. If I detract from my focus on the bar, then I'll lose it and not have anything. Uncle Max did just fine being single. I wasn't lying when I said I was married to the bar. This place is my life and if I let one man upend everything I've worked for, I'll let my uncle down.

The night is cool. Cars are making their way home, getting ready to start a new work week. Me, I've got my car door open, ready to run from anything that could potentially make me happy. I throw the bank bag and my wallet on the passenger side seat. The second I bend to slide into the driver seat, I hear footsteps behind me. There is only one person I know who walks with that sort of determination.

Standing, I close the door and lock it. The deposit for the morning is in my front seat, and while I trust most of the people here, I don't want my lack of attention to get our earnings stolen. Instead of letting him corner me at my car, I walk in his direction. Stopping short when he sees me. Damn, did I just make this worse? He could be coming to his car. It's parked two spots over from mine. Maybe he took my words seriously and wanted to go home and get his own thoughts in order.

"Angie," his voice is a whisper on the Spring night. "I figured you would have peeled out of here already." He leads us against the wall. The shadow concealing us from anyone passing by. "I know this," he points between the two of us, "it's scary as hell. Believe me, I thought about not confronting you. But I had to know. You turning me down those years ago was because I was still a kid in many ways. I'm not that kid anymore. I *need* for you to see that."

"You're crazy if you think I don't." I can't even be around him without undressing him with my eyes or seeing how he interacts with people. The tenderness he shows despite his size or how undeserving he feels he is. "It's taken everything in me not to react to you. My biggest fear is you coming in the way of what I've built and what I'm continuing to build."

"Understandable, but you realize I wouldn't do that, right?" He moves until he's directly in front of me, my back against the brick wall. "I have too much respect for you to let that even be an option."

"You say that now," my voice catches in my throat and I clear it. "But if we were to start dating, or whatever it is you want to do, and it ends badly, you might feel differently. You can't promise something now and know, one hundred percent that's the way it's going to turn out in the end." He has to see that. He has to know that I'm not coming at this from a bitter place. I'm being logical.

Leaning forward, he braces his hands on the wall on either side of me. "That goes the same for you." He brings one hand back to lift my chin until I'm looking into his eyes. "You can write off what *could* happen between us because you're scared of how it could turn out. I know you want the promise that I'll stay here, and I can't give that to you. We could do the whole long-distance thing if we have to. But that's a problem for *future* us. It's okay to live in the moment. To not know what's going to happen from one day to the next. I know you do that for the most part, but you also need to it with your heart." He points to my chest as if I don't know where my heart is. But he doesn't touch me. Always the gentleman.

"Statistically long-distance relationships never work." There, maybe that will shut him up.

"True, but we aren't at that point yet. We don't even have to define ourselves as a couple. That's not what I'm after." He pauses for a second and shakes his head. "That's not even on my radar. Right now, I want to see how compatible we are. If things go well, we can label it, but until then we can go with the flow. Can you do that?"

He speaks with such passion. I imagine he's been practicing this since his failed attempt at eighteen. Though, I take partial blame for that. The guy I was dating was a total douche and made him feel horrible. I didn't even get a chance to say anything before he rushed off my porch. That guy didn't last long. Once I knew Dylan was gone, I told him to leave and not bother asking for a second date. I don't date assholes. I do, however, want to get to know this side of Dylan. The one who is sure of himself and unafraid to back down. Despite my fears, I say the one thing that's bound to turn my world upside down. "Yes."

That was what he needed to hear, and he doesn't hesitate to make his move. He walks forward until the brick is digging into my back. The rough scrape a perfect contrast to his lips on mine. One of his hands is still on the wall, creating a barrier to the outside world, and the other is tangled in my hair, tilting my head back for better access.

The kiss is slow, tentative, unsure of how much I'll allow him to take of me. For all his confidence, he still needs me to direct the pace. I press myself into him, our bodies touching at multiple points. My lips part wider, granting him entrance. Letting his tongue dance with mine to a rhythm only we can hear.

Even though my eyes are closed, I can hear cars as they pass by the bar. Hopeful none of them can see us. Dylan's hand releases my hair and slides down my neck, soft and tender despite his appearance. A few caresses with his thumb then his hand runs down my back, landing at my hip, pulling me even closer to him. Not an inch of space between us.

I pull back for a moment needing to see his face. See if this is truly happening, or if it's something we've both daydreamed. Back then, I never considered him to be more than a friend. He's ten years younger than me. Now, it's much less of an issue. Now he's a man. One that wants me as much as I want him in this second, if the bulge in his pants is any indication.

Done with my perusal, I pull him back to me, his lips smashing into mine and sparks flying behind my eyelids. In all the years I've been kissed by various guys, nothing compares to this. His hand slides down to my ass, lifting me up to wrap my legs around his hips. For a split second I forget where we are. Forget that we're technically on the main road and anyone can see us. A car honking its horn shatters the illusion.

I unwrap my legs and slide down him until my feet are on the ground. This was stupid. That could have been one of my customers. Or, worse, one of the nosy ladies in town that spreads gossip like it's currency. This. This is why me and him is a bad idea. When he's around I lose all sense of the world around me and focus solely on him.

"I can't do this." I duck under his arm and rush to my car. To my surprise he doesn't follow me. Only stares in wide-eyed wonder as I start my car and reverse out of the parking spot. Am I running away like a scared child? You bet your ass I am, but I need time to think. To process what we could potentially work without him, and his mouth, around clouding my judgment.

* * *

My house is quiet when I get home. Not that it should be a surprise, but it would be nice to come home to someone. To have someone share my burdens with. With the door locked behind me, I head to the kitchen and grab the bottle of whiskey out of the freezer. Maybe the cold soothing liquid will knock some sense into my head.

I pull a shot glass out of the dish drain and fill it to the top. What I really wish I had was someone I could talk to about this. Not my mom because she would go on and on about how dating someone, I used to babysit, would shed negative light. Lisa will be doing her best to set us up on dates. She thinks I haven't noticed the excitement in her eyes when she looks at me and Dylan, but she's getting almost as bad as Stella. And I'm definitely not calling her.

Carlos is an option, though after walking in on me and Dylan kissing today, probably not the best one. There's only one person I know will be brutally honest with me, and give me advice.

I grab my phone out of my pocket and hit the second number under my favorites. It rings three times before there's an answer. "Well, Sis, it's been a minute. To what do I owe the pleasure?"

Ugh, my brother can be a pain in the ass. Maybe I shouldn't have called him after all. "You know what, never mind."

I'm about to hit end, but his voice comes through the receiver. "No, wait. I'm sorry. It's just that you call so rarely, I didn't know what to expect." He's not wrong. "And I haven't seen you in a while. Everything okay?" Dammit, I need to make more of an effort to see the family. With more employees, I can do it again.

"Sorry," I hold the phone between my ear and shoulder, grab the liquor bottle and shot glass and head toward the living room. My couch has seen better days, but I can't complain. It's not like I'm ever really home to use it. The TV even has a thin layer of dust on it. I forget what it's like to come home and relax. Even though the bar closes early on Sundays, I'm typically there until late at night working on admin things. "Things have been a little nuts at Out of the Ashes. I'll try to do better about checking in."

"You mean with the expansion project and all the new employees you've just hired?"

"How did you know?"

"Ang, just because I live on a ranch outside of town doesn't mean news doesn't make its way to me. Besides, I like to keep my ear to the ground and see what you're up to since you don't call or come around."

Way to call me on my bullshit. "Again, I'm sorry about that." I debate turning on the TV, but I need to focus on a conversation with my brother. "There is a reason I called, though."

"There usually is," he sighs. "Hit me with it. Whatever it is, it can't be that bad."

"Actually, it might be a little shocking." I wince. I don't know why, it's not like he can see me. "You remember that kid I used to babysit and cart all around town?"

"Dylan Knight? Yeah, I remember him, he did some work out here for a few summers to earn some cash. Did something happen to him?" I hear the panic in his voice. I wasn't the only with a soft spot for him. It's also good to know that he doesn't hear *everything* that goes on in my bar.

"No, nothing happened to him. He's actually back in town and working at the bar." I wait for a response, but he doesn't say anything. "But there's one other thing..."

"Let me guess, he still harbors a crush?"

Weird. "Okay, you going to have to stop that freaky mind reading thing."

"It's not mind reading, smart ass. It's common sense. He's had it bad for you since he was a teenager. It makes sense that he still does. Did he do something to make your uncomfortable?" His tone is hard. No matter how much he likes Dylan, nobody messes with his sister.

"Not at all, but he's made his feelings known, and I told him I'm attracted to him." I hear his throat clear on the other side. "And I may have made out with him."

"Shouldn't you be talking to someone else about this? Like a girl friend or something? I'm not sure I'm qualified."

Of course, he gets squeamish at that part. "I would but they are all dead set on making me and him a thing. I needed an outsider's perspective. You were the lucky one.

Can you imagine if I called Mom? I'd never hear the end of it." I pour another glass. If I know my brother, he's doing the same thing. Or, he might be drinking straight from the bottle. Who knows?

"Yeah, that wouldn't have gone over well." He pauses for a beat. "Do you like him? As in more than just wanting to jump his bones?" I can't believe he just said that.

"I think so. But what if it doesn't work out? Or I get distracted from the bar? Besides it's not like he's staying in town. He's here to help his mom while she's hurt." I know this sounds childish, but I seriously need the help.

"It sounds like you could use some distraction if you ask me. You spend way too much time tied to the bar. Take some time to enjoy life." I'm shocked. Speechless, even. It's not the advice I was expecting. "Ang, you there?"

It takes me a couple of seconds to register what he said. "Yeah. I'm just thrown for a loop, I guess. I didn't expect that from you. But maybe you have a point. He brought up the same things but also said it's a risk and I have to decide if I'm willing to take it. I told him yes, but the minute someone honked while we were outside, I ran."

"Please don't indulge on what you were doing. But he's right it's a risk and it's up to you." He sighs, "I can't tell you how to live your life, but this might be what you need. Distractions are good every once in a while. And if it doesn't last, and he leaves, at least you had fun."

"When did you get so wise," I laugh.

"I've always been. You just choose not to listen. At least consider it this time."

"I will. Thanks, brother. I'll come see you soon."

"You better, or I'll have to come steal you away for a weekend on the ranch. It's been a while." His chuckle is everything my childhood memories are made of. "Do something for you Angie, everything will work itself out one way or another."

"Absolutely. Love you." I hit the end button on my phone. With my brother on my side, I know what I have to do. But I'm not going to wait until he comes to work. I'm going to take matters into my own hands.

14

dylan

LAST NIGHT WAS a total fucking bust. I thought for a split second we were on the same page. That Angie was going to give what we're feeling a real shot. But I was only lying to myself. Even after everything I said, she *still* doesn't see me. What do I have to do? Write it on a poster and stand outside the bar. Will that show her how serious I am? I don't understand why she's so adamant about running when all I want is a shot. No labels, no confessing undying love. Just a chance to show her that what I feel is real and not some dumbass fantasy.

Fear is what is holding her back. Fear of what us being together would look like to this small town that we owe absolutely nothing to. Fear of doing something that takes her away from her bar for five minutes. Fear of allowing someone in to support her other than her friends. Fear. It's what stops anyone from going after what they want. It's what held me back when I was younger until I decided I had to prove that I wasn't some poor kid. That I deserved to take up space. Fear isn't something I'm willing to live by.

"Dylan," Mom's voice is loud from her bedroom. She's started sleeping in there again. Apparently, the couch is too uncomfortable for her old body. I tried telling her she wasn't old, but she wasn't having it. "Can you go by the store before you head to work? I want to bake something, but I need a few things."

My feet carry me down the hallway toward her room. It's weird how much space I fill now, as an adult, than I did when I was a scrawny teen. "What all specifically do you need? I'm going to head out for a run before I go, if that's okay."

"Yes, silly boy, I'll have the list ready for you when you get back." I turn back toward the door. Ready for my feet to hit pavement. Anything to keep my mind off being completely dismissed by Angie...again. "Before you go, can you bring me some paper and a pen? I would get up, but I my foot is hurting today."

That's news to me. She hasn't mentioned it hurting at all the past few days. "Do I need to take you back to the doctor? Have you been using the walker like you're supposed to?"

"Of course," she scoffs. "Most of the time."

"What do you mean most of the time?"

"It's not always convenient when I need to go to the restroom, it takes a minute to get situated." She doesn't like being admonished by me, but right now I really don't care. "I'll be fine. I just need a little rest."

She's beyond stubborn, and I feel the need to stay with her twenty-four seven. She's clearly not doing what she's supposed to be doing while I'm at work. Maybe working at Out of the Ashes isn't that great of an idea. No matter that

I'm doing it for her, to make her life better in the future. "Okay, Mom," I sigh. "But we're going to talk about this later."

"I assumed as much," she waves me away, "go do whatever you need to. If you don't make it to the store before your shift, it's fine."

"Mom, I'm not running all day. That's insane. I don't even go in until later tonight." When she's asleep and should be up for anything else. "I'll be back in a bit." Leaning down, I kiss her forehead before walking out of her room.

I swear, if rejection from Angie doesn't completely deflate me, my mom not doing what she's supposed to will. At least I can understand why Mom is having a hard time. She doesn't like to be seen as weak. Being in a cast is already a blow to her ego, but being forced to stay off her leg...that hits her pride like nothing else. She's not used to being sedentary, and I can't completely blame her. But, if she doesn't listen to what the doctors tell her, she's going to be in the cast for longer than either of us wants.

A quick pit stop to my room for my air pods and I'm out the door. If I were home, I'd use the treadmill in the apartment gym to blow off steam. I can't do that here for obvious reasons. Mostly the fact we don't have one. My feet lead me along a familiar path. Down the street and to the alley. The same route I ran when I needed to think as a teen. Nobody, other than whoever is home at this time, can see me back here. It's the perfect hiding spot while working the frustration out.

Last night I had so much optimism. Hell, I even thought I might be able to come home and be happy. Today, it's a different story. Rejection burns like acid in my stomach. Add in the issues Mom is giving me and I don't know if I'm able to handle being in Asheville until Mom can be mobile.

* * *

Rock music is blaring through my air pods when I finally make it back home. I ran further than I used to down these roads. I was halfway to Brews Clues before I'd realized just how far I'd gone.

Sweat is dripping off my face when I open the door to my house, blurring my vision. Hopefully, Mom is feeling better and we can have a chat about using the damn walker. What I don't expect to see is mom sitting on the couch, talking to Angie. I didn't even realize she was here. I guess I was so focused on running that I missed seeing her car out by the road. A quick glance out the still open door behind me proves I did in fact not see her car parked by the curb.

"What are you doing here?" I don't have to say her name. She knows exactly who I'm talking to.

"Dylan," mom admonishes me, "is that any way to talk to a guest?" Not even in the slightest, but right now I really don't care. I had finally gotten her off my mind, and now she shows up to my house unannounced. Who the hell does that?

"No, Ms. Knight, it's fine." Angie's blushes. And if I wasn't so frustrated with her, it would be kind of cute. "He has every right to question why I'm here."

"Oh. And why is that?" Mom lifts an eyebrow as if she knows something neither of us are privy to.

"We have some things we need to talk about." Angie shrugs her shoulders as if it's no big deal.

"No," I shake my head. "We really don't. I think you made your intentions perfectly clear yesterday."

"That's actually what I came to talk to you about. If you'll give me the chance."

Mom looks between us as if we're a ping pong match and she's trying to keep her focus on the ball. "I think I should let you two talk."

"No, Mom. It's fine." I'm not exactly in the mood to talk right now. The run was working, and now all the momentary joy is gone. "Besides, don't you have groceries you need me to pick up. I can go do that right now."

"Don't be ridiculous. You are a mess. And there's no way I'm going to have my son go to the store looking like that." It would probably sting her pride, but everyone in this town has seen me in much worse condition. "Take whatever time you need to talk and then you can go to the grocery store. And if you don't make it, that's fine, too."

I don't miss the sly smile on her face. I'm just hoping she isn't coming up with some love story between me and Angie in her mind. That will never happen. As much as I wish it might. Angie is the one holding back. And I'm not sure I want to wait on her any longer than I already have.

I've told her how I feel twice. Both times I thought she understood. Especially after the last time. I thought for sure she was going to give us a shot. But I was wrong on both accounts. How does that saying go? Fool me once, shame on you, fool me twice shame on me. I think I'm at my limit. The only positive I see in this room right now is my mom using her walker to get around. Her knee is propped up on the little sitting area as she rolls toward her bedroom. I'm going to call that a win for today, and that's all that matters in the grand scheme of things.

"You look like a mess." I feel like that should have gone without saying. Of course, I look like rough. I just finished running for way longer than I expected. All because my mind was stuck on *her*.

"Do you want me to go change before we have this talk? Or maybe you could deny you're attracted to me some more and we can be done with it. That way, I only have to see you when I'm at work, and it'll be no pressure. I'll even work on the opposite shift that you do just so we can limit our interaction." Do I sound bitter? Yes. How am I not supposed to be? It might even be a little childish. But I don't care. Not right now, anyway. She left me standing outside of Out of the Ashes looking like a damn fool. She also just glimpsed how hurt I am.

"That's actually part of the reason I'm here." Angie sighs, "I had some time to think last night and there's no fighting this pull I feel toward you. As much as I try to deny it, I can't." That last part is almost a whisper. As if she hopes I don't hear it.

"And what exactly do you want me to do with that information, Angie?" I cross my arms and lean against the door jamb. I'm not getting close to her. Every time I do, my mouth winds up on hers. "You told me the same thing last night and then ran. Honestly, in a lot of ways, you're the one acting like the younger person and not me. So, what am I supposed to do with that?" It's a low blow. I know that as soon as the words leave my mouth, but I can't help it. I feel like that eighteen-year old boy all over again.

She looks down at her clenched hands in her lap. Squeezing them so tight they are almost red. "I guess I deserve that." Damn, the defeat in her voice makes me feel even worse for saying it. But I'm not going to apologize. Not yet. I need to know what else she's going to say. "Look, I'm not saying what I did was right. If I'm being honest, I'm terrified to start anything with you. Whether it's short term, or not, I can't stop thinking about you."

"At least you're admitting it now," I scoff, "so, what does this mean, exactly?" I refuse to be the one making the first move. Not again. Third time's a strikeout in my book. If she is being honest, then she needs to come to me. She needs to decide that I'm what she wants. I do, however, move closer to her. I sit on the couch opposite, and rest my elbows on my knees. "Me possibly leaving is a tomorrow problem. You and me, right here? That's a today problem. One I'd like to get solved before I lose my ever-loving mind."

She turns to see if my mom is visible before facing me again. "It's going to be hard to automatically stop worrying about what people are going to think. But," she pauses for a second and lets out a breath, "I'm willing to give it a shot. For real this time. No more running away because I'm scared."

She doesn't move a muscle, waiting to hear what I'm going to say. After the past twenty-four hours, I think I want to let her stew for a bit. It might make me an asshole, but I want to be sure before I go all in. Rejection isn't something I deal with easily, and nobody knows that. The only person that might have a clue is Marshall. He was the only one that bothered checking in on me when we were kids. Even when I went off to college, he'd send me random texts. I may have a thing for Angie, but I'm not putting that much trust into her. Not yet.

"Okay, we'll take this slow." When she raises her eyebrow, I can't help but chuckle. "Slowish," I amend. "Why don't we have lunch before going to work? It doesn't have to be in public...yet. I have to get groceries for my mom, but if you're willing, I can bring food to your place."

"But I need to be at the bar when it opens," she argues. I lean back into the couch and cross my arms. "Fine," she rolls her eyes. "Carlos is perfectly capable of opening the bar. Half of the new hires are working today and since it's Monday, it shouldn't be too busy."

"See," I uncross my arms. "Problem solved. So, you, me, lunch?"

"Yes," she stands. "Be at my house in an hour and a half?"

"Wouldn't miss it," I grin and stand as well. I walk her to the door. "What do you want to eat?"

Once I pull it open, she steps out and looks over her shoulder. "Since you know me so well, surprise me."

Okay, that's how she wants to play it. My eyes are on her ass as she walks to her car. I rush to the shower now that she's pulled away. I hope like hell Mom's grocery list isn't too long.

15

angie

I SHOULD NOT BE this nervous. It's also the first time I've spent more than a few waking moments in my house. The house smells like lemons and laundry. The dust on the TV last night is no longer there. The dishes have been cleared from the sink, and candles are burning on the coffee table. The last thing I want him to think is I don't have a life outside the bar. Even if it is true. My brother was right, I need to take more time for myself.

I hear Dylan's car pull into the driveway before I see it. Rushing to the mirror in the hallway, I check my hair and makeup. Rarely do I wear it outside of work. I wouldn't even have it on then, but since the night scene has picked up, you get better tips when you have on makeup. The only thing I didn't add is the bright red lipstick. Maybe I should add it to my armor, though. I'm completely out of my element here.

Knock. Knock. Shit, he's actually here. My heart skips a

beat, and there's a small part that wants nothing more than to ignore him and pretend I'm not here. But the other part...that one calmly makes her way to the door. Deep breath in and out. My hand is over the knob and I turn it. "Hey." Fuck. Did my voice just go all high and airy? I don't think I've ever done that. Not even when I was a teen. What the hell is wrong with me? Not that anyone would blame me. Dylan's jeans are tight and hug him in all the right places. He's changed to a shirt that displays all the muscles I'm sure are trying to hide underneath. A backward baseball cap covers his head. I'd be lying if I said the whole look wasn't panty melting.

"Hey back." He grins. He stands awkwardly at the door, peering around me. "Are you going to invite me in? Or, are we going to eat right here?"

Yep, this boy is going to break me. Whether I agreed to whatever this is, or not, he was always going to be a temptation. "Yeah, come in. Sorry, I, uh, lost my train of thought for a second." Dear God, did I just say that out loud? What the fuck? He shows up looking like sex on a stick, and I've lost all capacity to think, or talk, like an adult. I'm in for a world of hurt.

"I bet," he smirks. "Where do you want me to put this?" He holds up a big bag from my favorite Italian restaurant. His other hand his behind his back, and I need to know what he's holding.

"You can set it on the table." I point toward the kitchen. For a split second I think I'm going to get a glimpse of what else he has, but he moves his arm as he passes me. It sounds like plastic rustling, though. The soft crinkle loud in my too quiet house. Music. That's what I need to turn on. Anything to fill the void. "What else do you have?" I lean on my tiptoes. My attempt to see over his shoulder is futile. He's too tall.

He continues keeping whatever is concealed as he sets the bag on the table. The front door is still open and I turn to close it. Before I can take a step in his direction, he's standing in front of me. The mystery item now in between the both of us. "These are for you."

I wrap my hands around the bouquet. They are exactly like the ones he tried to give me all those years ago. When I thought he was a kid, and he wanted to prove that he was mature enough to date someone ten years older than him. "They are beautiful. Thank you."

Lifting them to my face, I sniff them. I mean it's customary. I think it is, anyway. Not many guys have gone out of their way to bring me flowers. Until this very moment, I didn't know how much I would appreciate the gesture.

"You act like you've never gotten flowers before." He's staring at me as if I'm a strange creature that needs sympathy.

"That's because I haven't." I don't know if I should be ashamed of this, or just roll with it because the types of guys I've dated in the past weren't too keen on giving me any. I've never really gotten the point of flowers. They're already dead when they're put into the bouquet, but they do brighten things even if they're in the process of decay.

"Seriously?" He asks. He grabs my hand and pulls me toward the kitchen. It's not like it's hard to miss. This house is tiny. "Do you have any tall glasses or a vase we can put them in?"

Honestly, I don't know if I want to put them in a vase. They are perfectly fine in my hand. This is quite possibly the sweetest gesture anyone has ever done for me. "I don't think so. But if push comes to shove, I have some glasses I use for Long Island tea. If that will work."

"Yeah, that should work. But don't be shocked if I buy you something pretty to put them in."

"You really don't have to do that. I very rarely have flowers in the house."

"Well, you better get used to having them around more often." He opens up cabinets, looking for something to put them in. I still don't want to let them go.

"Why is that?"

"Because my mom told me the way to court a woman is to bring her flowers. It's what my dad did for her. And it's something she instilled in me." I don't miss the grimace after he mentions his dad. He bailed on them shortly after Dylan was born. At least that's what I overheard when my parents were talking about it. They didn't think I was listening when I was a teen myself and taking the job of watching Dylan.

"Well, I guess I'll just have to get used to flowers then." I take one last sniff before handing them over to him. "As long as they're bright. Don't bring any dark, broody things in here. It'll ruin the vibe."

His laugh is rich and deep. "There isn't much of a vibe to ruin in here, Angie. I'm pretty sure I have more style in my one bedroom apartment than you have in your entire house. It feels sterile."

"Geez, don't sugarcoat it or anything." I'm not sure if I should be offended or not. It's not my fault it's not decorated and homey.

"Sorry," he laughs again. "I didn't mean it to come off that way. It just looks like nobody lives here."

"That's because I'm always at the bar." I don't know

how many times I need to tell people this before they believe me. That place is my life.

"You've had this place since I was a teenager. How do you still have nothing up in it?"

"Again," I shrug. "I'm always at the bar. If I could, or if it wouldn't be seen as weird, I would probably have a twin size mattress in the office. So, I can catch some sleep on the really late nights."

"Are you serious?" He steps back to study my face. "You're at the bar that much? How do you have any time to do anything you *like* to do?"

"I don't know. There isn't a whole lot I like to do outside of making sure the bars is successful." It almost feels like I'm in an interrogation. Any minute he'll start playing good cop, bad cop.

"Look Angie, I'm saying this as someone who's trying to be your friend, not as the guy that wants to get in your pants. You need a life. And I mean that in the best way possible. You need something to look forward to that doesn't bring you stress. Something you do for pure enjoyment without a care in the world." He takes three steps to the table and pulls the chair out for me to sit. "I promise I'm not trying to be an asshole."

I know it's not coming from a place of malice, but I can't help defending my choices. "I *do* enjoy spending my time at the bar." I sit down and wait for him to take his seat. "It's stressful at times, but it's my happy place. It's the only place I feel close to Uncle Max." Whoops. I didn't mean to say that part. Even my parents and brother don't know that. It slipped out without me noticing until I'd already said the words. Dylan demolishes the walls I keep up without even trying.

"Oh," he clears his throat. "I'm sorry, I didn't realize."

Dammit, I killed the mood without meaning to. This is the other reason I don't date. I suck at it. You see those memes on social media that say ruin a date with four words, and all I have to do is open my mouth. "It's okay," I sigh. "Nobody knows. They didn't have the relationship I had with him. I always knew the bar would be mine." I grab the containers out of the bag and wait for him to tell me which one is mine. "I only thought he'd be here when we made it amazing."

Dylan grabs both containers and pops them open. His holds a massive slice of lasagna, and mine is full of spaghetti. "You know he's proud of you, right? He'd be amazed at everything you've accomplished." He slides my container in front of me and hands me silverware.

Patrick does an amazing job cooking up goodies at the bar, but it's nice to have a meal that isn't on my own menu. Twirling the fork in the noodles, I think over his words. "I know he would be. It's hard sometimes because I can't pick up the phone and call him with ideas. It's the main reason Stella handles a lot of the renovation. She gets it without having to be told." I take a bite, chewing and swallowing until my mouth is no longer full. "I can say the simplest thing and she can run with it. The pain of him not being here is easier handled this way."

"If I'd realized, I never would have opened my mouth. I'm sorry for bringing up painful moments." He uses a knife to cut a piece of the lasagna after struggling with the fork. "Talk about bringing down the mood."

"You're fine." I give him a reassuring smile. At least, I hope it is. Not many people understand. They didn't spend all their free time in the bar. "So, since you brought up the subject, what do you do for fun? Hell, what do you even do for a job when you aren't here?" I just realized I never asked when he turned in his application.

"I'm a mechanic," he shrugs. "It comes easily to me and I enjoy it. There's something about being under the hood of a car. You find a problem and try to solve it." He takes another bite of his food.

"Why the hell didn't you ask Johnny for a job? You realize he runs Small Town automotive now, right?" I need a drink. If I didn't have to drive, I'd make it liquor. Anything to get through most awkward date in the history of my life. Maybe I'm the one making it that way, but I'm severely out of practice. I stand and head to the fridge. With the door open, I let the cool air hit me in the face. Anything to bring down my nerves. I grab a bottle of water for me, and lift one, waving it at Dylan. He nods his head and I rejoin him at the table.

"I think we both know the reason." He winks and continues eating. Like he didn't just admit to only asking for a job to be closer to me.

"And that's the only reason?" Yes, I'm digging. If I'm going to see where this thing goes, I need to get to know who he is *now*.

"It's most of the reason." Now he's the one shrugging. "You do need someone there to handle the riffraff when it comes in. Seemed like the perfect job for me to pass some time and earn some money while I'm here."

"In case you haven't noticed, that was pretty much a one time thing. Nobody else has caused issues since." The spaghetti is delicious and I'll be surprised if I don't have red splatters all over my clothes. In all honesty, this meal should come with a bib.

"Yeah," he snorts. "That's because I'm there. You know

how people in this town talk. As soon as word spreads, shit like that cuts way down."

He's not wrong, even if he's a little too cocky about it. Anytime there's been break-ins, someone mentions security cameras and the magically stop. Probably because the teenage punks doing it are scared one of their friends is going to snitch. The joys and wonders of living in a small town.

Wait a minute. That's not the biggest reason he gave me when he asked for the job. "I thought you wanted a job to put back money for your mom. You could have banked a hell of a lot more with Johnny. Was that a lie?"

He sets his fork down and leans back in the chair. "No, it wasn't. I hate the thought of her working two jobs. If the money I'm putting back will help her quit at least one of them, I'll be happy."

"See," I smirk. "I wasn't the only reason. Though you'd still make more with Johnny."

Dylan grabs his container and stands. Scooting around the table to the kitchen. "Where's the trash can?" Huh, he even cleans up after himself. That's a far cry from the little Dylan I used to babysit. It was a nightmare getting him to do his chores. It's nice to see he's grown up in that aspect.

"It's in the cabinet by the sink." I point to the lower left. I close my box and get up to put it in the fridge. "Thank you for lunch. It was really good. How did you know this was my favorite?"

He closes the cabinet after tossing his container in the trash. "Angie, I've been paying attention to you for well over a decade. I probably know you better than anyone else."

I snort. "That doesn't sound creepy at all." The clock on the microwave catches my eye and I can't believe how much time has passed since he's been here. "Shit. I need to get to the bar."

"Why?" He's leaning against the sink and doesn't move a muscle at my announcement.

"Because I still have things I need to do." It doesn't take him two seconds to cross the space and place his hands on either side of me. Oh shit. I've backed myself into a corner. Except, I don't know if I want to be set free.

16

dylan

ANGIE SUCKS in a breath as I close the distance. Is it fear? Or anticipation? Either way I'm going to find out. "You just can't stand it, can you?"

"Wh—what do you mean?" Her chest heaves and I lean in. Waiting to see how close she's going to let me get before she tries to push me away.

"Being at the bar. It's like this need that drives you. I know you said you feel closer to your uncle, but I think it's something else, too."

Her eyes widen, but her back straightens. She's not going to let me push her around. "Like what?" Her arms fold in front of her chest.

I pause for one. Two beats. Watching her squirm has become one of my favorite past times these couple of weeks. Normally, I'm a gentleman. I can turn the charm on and off, but I'm not letting her scurry away so easily. Not this time. "Like hiding from anything real. If you're completely caught up in work, you don't have to go after anything. You can have a simple life without giving into any of your desires."

"Who says I desire anything?" She scrunches her nose. My words are absolutely ludicrous to her.

This time I don't back down. I step closer to her, barely any space between us. Our stances mimicking last night. The only difference, we have no audience here. No cars passing by, or lurkers trying to figure out what we're doing. It's just me and her. "Your eyes don't lie, Ang. You can deny it all you want, but the way you're trying to pretend you're not checking me out speaks volumes."

She opens her mouth to argue. But I don't give her the chance. Faster than she realizes what is happening, my hands go to her waist and I lift her on the counter. Her legs on either side of me. Her mouth an "o" of shock. "Tell me right now you're not trying to escape anything real that could happen between us. That you're going purely for managerial reasons, and I'll let you go. But if it's a cop out, let me know."

She sits in silence. Her eyes bouncing everywhere around the room. Anything to avoid looking at me. I don't blame her. There's nothing that gets under Angie's skin more than being put on the spot. Normally she can talk her way out of things. Not today, though. If we're going to give this thing a fair shot, she's going to be honest with me. I think I deserve that at least.

With nowhere else to look, her eyes finally meet mine. "It's a cop out, okay," she huffs. "I don't know how to react around you. As much as I want to see how you look without that shirt, I'm terrified I've forgotten how to be with someone."

"It's a good thing I'm not just *someone*." I lift an arm and reach over my head. Grabbing the back of my shirt, I pull it off with one hand. "And now you don't have to wonder what I look like with it off."

Her gasp is worth it, and the barely audible sound makes my blood rush south. As much as I want her right this very moment, I won't do anything until she gives me the go ahead. She shakes her head. To clear her mind, or rid herself of the image, I don't know. "I don't remember you always being this cocky." She grins, and for once things seem to be going my way.

Shrugging, I step closer. There's no room between us, and she leans back to look up at me. "I told you...I grew up."

In an almost trance like state, she lifts a hand and touches my shoulder. Then she's running her fingers down my chest. The slow pace is a sweet, sweet torture. So many times I've imagined a moment just like this, and it's finally become a reality. "Tell me something I don't already know."

Bending down until my mouth meets her ear, I whisper, "I want you."

A shiver runs through her and she sucks in a breath. There's no denying I have as much of an effect on her as she does me. "Me too." Those two words are the most amazing thing I've ever heard, but she's not done. "Now, what are you going to do about it?"

Fuck. Being a gentleman has flown right out the damn window. That's the invitation I was waiting for. The confirmation I needed. Without hesitation, I pull her toward me. My mouth slamming onto hers. Her arms wrap around my neck and her legs circle my waist. There's no way she doesn't feel how much I want her, and I hope like hell I don't freak out and underperform. She deserves so much better than that.

She's clinging to me like I'm the water she needs to survive in a desert. My lips move from hers, and I kiss across her jawline until I reach her ear. Between nibbles along her lobe, I ask, "Bedroom?"

Please don't deny me. Not now that we are both getting what we want after fighting it longer than we should have. She doesn't disappoint. A sharp exhale and a nod. I lift her off the counter and carry her out of the kitchen. "That way," she nods her head toward the back of the small house before placing rushed kisses along my neck. Each one a promise of what's to come.

"I know where you room is," I grunt. "I used to come here after practice, remember?" Maybe I shouldn't have said that. It may very well pull her out of the moment and into her own head, worrying about our age difference.

Instead, she laughs softly. "Oh yeah, you don't forget anything." It's hard to when she's always been the one, I held out for. Not to say I don't have fun when I'm home, but I always knew if I got the chance with her, I'd take it.

I shift one hand to her ass to keep her balanced while I open the door to her room. Once inside, I kick it closed with my foot. Why? I don't know. It's not like anyone else is here, or might walk in. She locked the front door after I came in, even if she didn't think I noticed. There was only one way this afternoon was going to end. With me between her legs. Deep down, I think she knew that.

The bed is on the other side of the room and I cross the short distance, easing her onto the bed. She pulls away from me. Her hands moving to the hem of her shirt, but I stop her. "No."

"What do you mean, no?" The frustration in her voice is amusing, and I know she's antsy. "That's typically how these things work, unless..." Her voice trails off and it takes me a second to realize what she's suggesting.

"God, Angie. I'm not a virgin." A blush takes over her

cheeks, and she shrinks back at her wrong conclusion. "I'm going to do it. I'm going to cherish, and enjoy, every fucking minute with you."

Not a word spills from her lips for a moment. She leans back on her hands and grins. "Well, I'm waiting." She doesn't even know how that one statement affects me. It's going to make going slow hard as hell.

I get down on my knees and I'm eye level with her now. The need for her to see me while I undress her is something I never thought would matter. With her, it does. My hands slide up her slender legs until I reach her thighs, and I pull her toward the edge of the bed. How's this for waiting? My fingers make their way to her shirt and I slowly lift it up. My mouth meeting the exposed skin as I lift it up and over her head.

My mouth hovers over her lace covered nipple and I suck through the fabric. One of her hands moves to the back of my head and presses me closer. A gentle bite is how I reward her, and she gasps. Reaching around her back, I undo her bra and toss it to the side. I sit back a moment and admire the beautiful woman before me.

Her hands reach out to pull me toward her again, but I don't let her. I reach down and unbutton her shorts. My fingers fumbling while I try to keep my cool. Why don't these things have a fucking zipper? When the last button is undone, Angie lifts up and I pull the shorts along with the panties down her legs, letting them fall in a pile on the floor.

"This isn't fair, Dylan," Angie sighs. "You are still half clothed and I'm buck ass naked."

"You are fucking gorgeous." It's not the response she wants, but it's all I can give. Never in my wildest dreams did I think I would have her in front of me like this. Wanting me just as much as I want her.

"Thanks, but if you don't do *something* I'm going to take over." Her voice is tight, barely containing the tension I'm sure is wracking through her body.

She can be bossy at work, but it does not compare to the words coming out of her mouth right now. And honestly, part of me wants to be dominated by her, but not until I take care of her first.

I pull her forward to the edge of the bed and gently push her back until she's lying down. Standing, I hover over her and take in all that she is. Absolutely perfection. She tries to fumble with the button of my jeans, but I press my mouth to hers, and the motion stops.

With one hand, my finger travels a path from her collarbone, between her breasts, and further down until I cup her wet pussy in my hand. I dip two fingers between her folds and thrust in and out. Honestly, if this feels like ecstasy to me now, I can't imagine what it's going to feel like when I'm actually inside her.

Angie breaks the kiss and whispers my name. "Dylan. I need you."

Her wish is my command. Slowly, I trail my lips down her body until my mouth is between her legs. I don't stop fucking her with my fingers as my tongue swirls around her clit.

Her moaning only intensifies, and her breathing is quicker. I know she's close to losing it, but I'm not going to let her come...yet. I pull back and slide my fingers from the between her legs, waiting for her reaction. She doesn't disappoint. She sits up and glares at me. "What the fuck are you doing?"

"Sweetheart, the first time I make you come, I want to be inside you. With no hesitation, her hands shoot out almost faster than I can see. Within seconds she has my jeans unbuttoned, the zipper down, and she's shoving them down my legs. She's as ready as I am, and I love that she's not afraid to go after what she wants. Especially now that she's giving us a shot.

Before long, she's stripping my boxers down as well. Now, I'm on full display for her. Standing, she forces me to take a step back. and grabs my shoulders, spinning me around until I'm the one against the bed. "You lay down now." Well, I guess I teased her too long, and now she's not giving me a choice. I do as I'm told, and lay down, waiting for her to take control. The thing she feels she needs in all things, not just her bar.

She leans on the bed, one knee to one side of me and an arm beside my face, bracing herself. Her other hand sliding up and down my cock. Teasing me just as much as I was teasing her. It's not as much fun when the shoe is on the other foot. "Dammit, Angie, I need inside you."

See grins and let's go of my cock, straddling me before she slides down. And, oh my god, I feel like I'm going to come in seconds. I grab on to her legs, hoping she gets the message to go slow. I'm not exactly sure how I pictured this scenario, but fuck it's better than anything I ever imagined.

Her pussy grips me tight as she begins rocking. Riding me like I wish she had done so many times throughout my teen years. She would have ruined me for anyone else. As much as I want this to last as long as possible, that's not going to happen. Not right now, anyway. Now...I need her moving fast and steady. My hands move to her hips, gripping them tight. Forcing her to move at a quicker pace. Her hands on my chest, fingers on my chest digging in. I know for sure there's going to be nail marks tomorrow. Right now, I don't care.

My entire body tenses and I know this is it. This is the

moment. She leans down, capturing my lips with hers and that's all it takes. I always thought it was cliche in movies when the girls said it felt like an explosion. But it's not inaccurate. It's like the Fourth of July behind my eyelids as I lose myself in her. Before I'm done, she's coming apart on top of me. It's like we're meant to do this. To experience this. To experience each other. And I hope like hell this isn't the last time.

After a few moments, she climbs over me and lays down beside me. "Next time you want to try to take control. Don't be such a tease." She pokes me in the ribs with her finger and starts laughing. "It's not so fun being on the receiving end, is it?"

I wrap an arm around her and pull her to me. "Maybe not, but it was worth it." We stay cuddled up for a few minutes and now I don't even want to go to work. The *only* thing I want to do is spend the rest of the day in this bed with the girl of my dreams.

17

angie

MY PHONE RINGS and I sit up in my bed. Well, I attempt to. It takes me a few moments to remember why I'm in bed, and then I look over. Dylan's arm is still wrapped around my waist, which makes it difficult to move.

What time is it? The last thing I remember is screwing his brains out and then nothing. We must have fallen asleep. I reach around Dylan and pull my shirt off of my alarm clock. He couldn't have just like laid it down on the floor so that it was within reach when we were done? I swear he has no aim.

The red numbers stare at me and holy shit. It's four o'clock and I'm still at home. Dylan is supposed to come in for his shift in a few of hours, and he's currently passed out in my bed. I cannot believe we fell asleep. Being with him is already making me shirk off my responsibilities to the bar.

Slowly pulling out of Dylan's grasp, I grab my shirt and throw it on over my head. He hasn't stirred once since I started moving around. I climb out of bed to look for something to cover my ass. It doesn't really matter because we're the only two here, but I can't remember if I closed blinds in the kitchen or living room. And I don't want anybody peeking in and getting a glimpse of me in all my naked glory.

Now that I'm fully dressed and Dylan is still asleep in my bed, I make my way to the kitchen. It's the last place I remember seeing my phone. It's on the kitchen counter, the screen lighting up what the text messages. Holy shit. I have six missed calls, and text messages fill my screen.

Unlocking the phone, I go to the missed calls first to see who it may have been. My money is on Carlos. But I don't expect all the freaking calls from my mom. That's not good. I'll deal with her later. Like tomorrow, or when she phones again and I'm actually near it.

Now the text messages. They are mostly from Lisa. Ranging from 'Where are you?' 'Are you still alive?' 'Are you with Dylan? And my personal favorite, 'are you getting some right now?' This woman has zero filter. Whatever pops into her head pops out of her mouth. One day it's going to come back and bite her in the ass. I don't bother responding. She'll call and I'm not sure I'm ready to let the world know about me and Dylan.

I move on to the next message. It's a text from Carlos.

CARLOS

> I tried calling, but I'm going to assume you're busy. Or you've lost your mind since you've never been late to the bar. Or maybe even kidnapped. I'm beginning to wonder if someone has replaced you with a changeling. I know you had lunch plans but I'm guessing they went a little long. Call me whenever you get this and we'll see when you decide to come in.

ANGIE

> Yes, I'm fine. I'll be there in about an hour. Hopefully the building hasn't burned down without me.

That was surprising. I figured out of anybody, Carlos would be the most pissed that I wasn't there. Here I am enjoying myself for once. And they're stuck at the bar with a bunch of newly trained employees that probably still don't know their way around. If there was an award for shitty, or absentee boss, I'd get it. Without a doubt.

I must be truly out of my mind. This cannot happen on a regular basis. Lunch plans? Yes. Amazing sex? Hell yes. But not right when before I'm supposed to go into work. That is where the problem lies. And I have a feeling it's where it will continue to lie if we keep this up.

"Hey," Dylan wraps his arms around me from behind. Even though I'm in the middle of a freak out about us, it's nice to be held by someone. "Is everything okay?"

"Carlos texted me and my mom called like a million times." I lean into him, letting him comfort me.

"The bar is fine, right?" There's a hint of concern, which is a good sign. It means he really understands the importance of it.

"Yeah," I nod. "I just feel like I need to be there. I basically threw all the new hires at Carlos and Lisa without asking if they were okay with it."

H doesn't say anything, and I wonder what he's going to say. A few more moments pass before he speaks. "I'll get out of your hair so you can go in. My shift starts soon anyway, and I want to stop and get Mom some food."

That's...not what I was expecting. If anything, I thought he would tell me to come back to bed. To skip off from work a little longer, ignoring all responsibilities. This just proves how much he's not like any other guy I've had a relationship with. Not that I've had many of those. Most of them lasted two or three weeks tops.

"Yeah, that sounds good." I turn around until his arms are behind me and I'm staring up at his eyes. "Thank you."

"Why are you thanking me?" He chuckles and shakes his head. "It's your job. I may have been a little pushy in getting you to admit your feelings, but I'm not an asshole."

"I never said you were," I lean into him. "It's just unexpected."

"Wow, if your thoughts of my reaction are so low, maybe you've been dating some real douchebags." He's not wrong. Most of them were not winners.

"I guess it's a good thing you aren't one, huh?" I feel his chin rest on the top of my head, but he doesn't say anything. Only pulls me toward him, hugging me. I let him for a few more seconds before pushing away. "But if I'm going to get to the bar in a decent amount of time, I need to get ready. Just had sex chic isn't exactly professional." I motion to my outfit.

"Go get ready." He moves to let me pass him. "I'll let myself out."

Going up on my tiptoes, I give him a quick peck. "I'll

see you at work in a few hours." As I walk away, he smacks my ass. Normally, I'd hate that shit, but with him...it's different. It feels the way new love, should.

* * *

It only takes me thirty minutes to get ready and to the bar. There's a reason I chose my house, even way back then when Uncle Max was alive. It's close to the bar and I can be there in a moments notice no matter the day.

The parking lot is filling up, and I know it's going to be a busy night. I hope the new hires are ready. Eventually I need to learn their names. I feel shitty calling them new hires all the time, but I want to make sure they are going to stick around.

I bypass the line of people waiting to get in. It's insane this old hole in the wall bar is now *the* place people want to be. Lisa is grinning like the cat who caught the canary when I open the front door. Her eyebrows lift up and down in a seductive manner. I hold my hand up to her when she opens her mouth. "Don't even say anything."

"I wasn't," she laughs. "You just said all I need to know with those four words." She doesn't see me roll my eyes because her attention is already on the next people in line.

The other space can't open fast enough. We *need* it more than anything right now. If folks have to spend long amount of time in line, they are going to find other bars to frequent. I can't let that happen. Not when Out of the Ashes is blowing up the way it is. Who knows, maybe we can even turn into a chain. Those are big dreams and would mean everything to me. Even with the added headache I'm sure it will be.

I make my way across the crowded room, and notice

Carlos grinning at me from behind the bar. "Look who finally decided to come in." He grabs a liquor bottle off the shelf and begins mixing a drink. "I'm sure hell must have frozen over for you to have missed most of the day. I hope it was worth it."

The last part of that statement was a dig, and I recognize it for what it is. He may have been okay with my disappearing act today, but he clearly still has issues with Dylan. If he knew him better, I think those fears might ease. I know he's only looking out for me...but I have a brother for that. I only need Carlos to be my friend.

"It was, thank you very much." My smile is wide, and I'm sure I look nuts, but I don't care. I told Dylan I'd give me and him a fair shot. That includes sticking up for how I spend my time.

He stares at me for a few seconds and nods. Acceptance even if he doesn't want to give it. This is why he's one of my best friends. When Stella finds out, that might be a different story. I'm sure she'd heard the whispers around the bar. I'm almost shocked her and Lisa haven't been planning a forced date between me and Dylan. Hell, for all I know they have been. But they don't know Dylan. Not like I do. He's persistent and unafraid to go after what he wants. It just so happened to be me he had his sights on.

I glance around on my way to my office. I'm certain I had more of the new people on the schedule than who is here. Surely if some didn't show up Carlos would have let me know. I continue down the hall. Actually, no he wouldn't. Even if I was with Dylan, he's probably happy I took some time for myself. Time away from here, even if only for a few more hours than normal.

My office is blessedly quiet when I open the door. A part of me wants to close the door behind me to think on how amazing sex with Dylan actually was, but I'm sure Carlos will come in here as soon as he has a moment. I set my bag on the table behind my desk and sit in the chair. It's not very comfortable, and I should replace it. I won't, though. It was Uncle Max's.

The work schedule is opened up on my desk. Either Carlos or Lisa already checked over it. Three names are crossed off. I knew there were more people scheduled to work today. At least some people decided they liked working here enough to come back a second day. That means more to me than they know. I pull the applications for the ones that didn't show up and set them aside. Those will go in a folder if they decide to reapply. Second chances are worth considering, but I like to keep tabs on who burned me once. My uncle would keep letting people come back even though they'd screw him over, and I'm not going to let that happen. It's not a good business model.

There's a knock on my open door, and I look up. Stella is leaning against the door, smiling. Oh shit, she knows. How the hell does she know? "What are you doing here? You never come to my office at night, you typically save that for the daytime. You know, protect that couple time for you and Johnny."

"I did come by earlier." She takes a few steps into the office and waits. "I was shocked to find out you *weren't* here. I don't think I've ever witnessed that before."

"A girl's allowed to have a little me time." I'm hoping that will be enough to keep her questions at bay. Too bad I'm wrong.

"Of course," she nods. "I figured I'd come in this evening to see how the new employees are working out."

"Fine. According to the schedule there were three no shows. So, I have a feeling they won't be back." I grab the applications and hand them to her. "I set these aside to put in your filing system."

"Thanks, but I heard from a little bird that you had a date." She claps her hands. "Any chance it was with Roger? Or, was it with the young new hottie in town?"

"Gross. Who says hottie anymore?" I feel like past a certain age you shouldn't be allowed to say it. "But, for your information, it was the latter. The guy you tried to set me up with was as dull as they come. I thought I told you that."

"No, you said not to set up any more surprise dates for you." She shrugs and takes a seat in the chair in front of my desk. "It looks like it's a good thing I didn't. Everyone could feel the tension you and Dylan give off. It's about time y'all did something about it. So, tell me, how did it happen?"

Do I really want to go down this road with her? We're not even an official anything. We're seeing how things go. Add in the fact that he's leaving once his mom is able to move on her own easier, it's pretty much a fling for while he's here. "He's persistent."

"That's all I get?"

"Yep." I lean back in the chair and almost fall out of it. Dammit. I'm going to have to replace this thing whether I want to or not. "I don't have to spill all my relationship details with you."

"Oh, so it's a relationship?" She scoots her chair closer to my desk.

"What? I didn't say that." Groaning, I run my hand over my face. Another knock on the door, and for a split second I think I'm saved from this conversation. Until I see who it is.

18

dylan

SO, what if I was listening in? I was curious to know what exactly she would say. Especially to one of her closest friends. That's usually when the actual truth comes out. She looks like she's struggling, though. As entertaining as it is, it looks like it sucks.

I tap against the open door three times, and Angie looks up. Shock written all over her face. "Am I interrupting?"

Both of them answer at the same time. Stella yells, "Yes." All the while Angie is shaking her head and gives a resounding "No." Honestly, I think it's a bit of both. Angie has to learn how to open up. If not to me, then at least to her friends.

"I'll just come back later." I start to turn around, ready to leave them to whatever conversation Stella is intent on having.

Angie's voice stops me in my tracks, much like it always does. "Wait." She glances at the old clock on the wall. The hands are almost bent at weird angles, and I'm not sure that it's going to work much longer. "Why are you here? You aren't supposed to come in for a two more hours."

"I passed by here when I was bringing my mom dinner. The parking lot was packed." I nod toward the main area of the bar. "I figured you might need more help. Too many hands is never a bad thing when it comes to serving food and drinks."

It's not the only reason. I *needed* to see her. To know that she was okay after today. To make sure she wasn't having doubts about any of it. Or worse, ashamed of being with me. With the way she's acting toward Stella's interrogation, there may be a bit of shame mixed in.

"Well, thank you for coming in early. We might actually need you since three people didn't show up." She's rubbing her temples, already stressed about her employees.

"Just tell me where you want me, and I'll go."

"Under her, over her, behind the desk," Stella mutters just loud enough for all of us to hear.

"Oh my God," Angie lays her head down on the desk. After a few moments, she pops back up. "Have you been body switched? I'd expect that comment from Tiffany, and not you."

"I guess she's rubbing off on me. We've been spending more time together since I've taken over planning her wedding." She sits up straighter. Obviously proud of what she's doing.

"Wow," I laugh. "You like to have your hands in everything, don't you?" That came out harsher than I intended and I wince once the words leave my mouth. "I'm sorry, I didn't—"

"It's okay," Stella gives me a small smile. "I'm good at what I do. There's a reason I was a project manager at one of the biggest firms in Austin. It's just more fun when I handle things for my friends and family. I get free rein and do what needs to be done."

"You aren't getting free rein of this place," Angie pipes up. "I mean, within reason. This isn't a big city bar."

"Don't be ashamed if that's what it turns into, Ang," I say, leaning against the door. "This place has a ton of potential, and I can see an Out of the Ashes sitting firmly in the downtown area of every major city."

Stella jumps to her feet, scaring the hell out of me. "I knew I liked you," she points at Angie, "you should keep him around. He's able to see the big picture."

Huh, I never considered it that way. But I guess I've always been that person who sees everything. It's what happens when I'm in a group of friends that nitpicked over the little things. They didn't see how those tiny moments were nothing compared to what the future held. I don't think I realized that until this moment.

Angie rolls her eyes at her friend, then meets my eyes. "Thanks, Dylan. Um, if you want to clock in, check in with Carlos and see where he needs you."

"Will do." I wave and walk back to the main bar. What the fuck? Why did I wave? I could have gone with a nod, thumbs up. No, not that either. This woman still makes me nervous despite us sharing a bed. I'm not a hundred percent sure how to meld both our worlds together, but I'll figure it out. Anything to stay a part of her world for as long as I can.

Carlos is pouring a drink when I head to the bar. "Angie said you might need some help up here. Just point me in the direction you need me."

He grunts, but doesn't answer. I'm not winning any ground with this guy. I don't know what I did to piss him off so much, but it's annoying. He finishes making the drink and waves me around to the opening by the computer.

"One of the new waitstaff is almost done with his shift, you can fill in for his tables." I turn toward the computer to clock in, but his hand lands on my arm. My first instinct is to throw my chest out, make myself appear bigger. Carlos isn't a big guy. Though I'm sure he could hold his own, and possibly kick my ass, if he has the right motivation. "Look kid, I don't know how long you're going to be here, but I do know one thing. Angie is one of the best people I know. She told me you had a boyhood crush on her. Don't let whatever it is you're doing with her be some game or fantasy you want to live out." I bristle, but he's not done. "If you're serious about her, you need to think about the future. I know you plan on leaving. Just know, that will have the potential to destroy her. When she loves, she loves hard."

He doesn't give me a chance to respond. He goes back to pouring drinks like he didn't just insult my character. What I feel for Angie is way more than some childhood crush. It was back then, too. But nobody ever believes a teenager. I've known what I wanted since then, and it never changed. Not even with the distance. I don't understand why certain people are making it a point to get into business that isn't theirs. His friendship with her doesn't give him a right to belittle me.

I take a deep breath and clock in. If I don't stay occupied, my thoughts will simmer and I'll just get pissed. Nobody tips pissy servers, and with the amount of people already showing up tonight, it's going to be a good one to earn some extra money. It doesn't stop the voice in the back of mind from whispering that I'm not wanted here...again.

* * *

I'm at the host stand, waiting for Lisa to call up the next guests. Even though we're packed in here, there's still a line of people waiting. Between the atmosphere and the menu, it's the highlight of the day for many of the folks in Asheville. Out of the Ashes is close to home and most of the folks that live in town can walk home if they aren't able to drive.

Lisa glances over at me while searching for the people whose name she just called out. "You okay?"

"Yeah, I'm fine," I grunt. "Why?"

"Maybe because your whole demeanor changed after you talked to Carlos?" She shrugs. "I may not know a lot about you, but I do know that you don't hide your emotions well."

"He said some things I didn't like."

"About you and Angie?" She does her best to keep her voice down, but the music is loud and I have to bend down to hear her.

"Something to that effect." Three people walk toward the stand and I sigh in relief. I don't want to get into the whole touchy feely spiel she has going on.

"Ignore him." She bumps my shoulder trying to force a smile. "He's just a grumpy old man." She squishes her nose. "Well, maybe not old, but he's definitely grumpy."

Once the group reaches us, I hold out my hand toward the room. "I'm Dylan and I'll take you to your table."

Whew. Saved by customers. Lisa is great to have as a friend, but if Stella is to be believed, she's the one who told her about me and Angie. I definitely don't want any of my business getting out. It's not bad, but way more than I can deal with. At least, not right now with a bar full of patrons.

I don't notice who else has been seated in my section until I finish up the order for the group I led to the table. When I turn around, Tonya is waving me over. "I heard a rumor you were working here," she shouts over the music.

"Yep," I nod. "Going on three weeks."

"I never pictured you working at a place like this. Well," she looks away. "I never pictured you doing anything but playing football." Looks like someone kept up with my college career after I left. It means she knows about the injury that flushed that future down the toilet.

"Honestly," I laugh, hoping it sounds real. The verbal punches just keep coming tonight. "It's not too bad. It keeps me busy while Mom is resting, and I make a little money."

"How is your mom doing?" She's looking at me again. No more pain on my behalf of my failed dreams. "Do y'all need help with anything?"

"Naw," I shake my head. "She's stubborn as usual. I have to stay on her about using her walker. She hates the damn thing."

"I can imagine," she laughs, "an independent woman like her won't let anything keep her down." She nods toward the other side of the room where Angie is taking an order. "But I imagine you know all about independent women."

For fucks sake, words moves fast around here. I remember why I hated living here as a teen. Everyone knew your business. "Why? What did you hear?"

"Nothing." She puts her hands up in surrender. "But I grilled her about you the night I took her to the care center. She definitely had a reaction to you. Did she finally make a move?"

"That's funny." I snort and almost choke. "She ran from

me twice when I opened up to her. But we're seeing how things go." I also forgot how easy it is to talk to Tonya. If you tell her something, it goes in a vault. Not a word repeated unless you give her the okay. Outside of Marshall she was probably the only other person I felt close to. When Jake dumped her in a horrific way, it ruined the friendship we had. We had to pick sides and Jake would have been hurt if I'd chosen hers. In a way she had a lot of things he didn't. He may have had money and a devil may care attitude, but it was all a front to how shitty his home life was. Even though I only had one parent, I knew I was loved unconditionally.

"I'm glad to hear it," she smiles. It only gets wider as she looks over my shoulder. I already know who it is before I turn around.

19

angie

"WHAT ARE YOU GLAD TO HEAR?" I do something I never thought I would do and link my arm into Dylan's. It's public confirmation of me and him being together. Even if we aren't labeling us. More shocking, this doesn't terrify me the way I thought it would. It feels natural. As if this is meant to be. Never have I imagined those thoughts popping into my head.

Tonya grins as she's looking at our interlinked arms. "That you finally got your head out of your ass and did something about your attraction to my friend,"

I don't miss the way Dylan stands taller. Or the smug look on his stupid face. "Well, it took some convincing, but I guess he's worth taking a chance."

"He's definitely worth it," Tonya laughs, "probably deserves it more than the rest of us." She's not wrong. Aside from her and the Marshall kid, the rest of them treated him like a commodity. Someone who was the tiebreaker whenever they would get in arguments.

I wonder if that is a part of the reason he left. There were no sad farewells. Or tear-stained cheeks. He came home after freshman year in college and then none of us saw him since. Not that I was keeping tabs or anything. But I guess you could say I had an investment in him, even back then. I needed to know that he was going to be okay, despite how he felt about himself. Things seemed to have worked out for him. From the car he's driving to the way he's taking care of his mom; I think he's doing very well for himself.

"We should probably get back to work." Yes, I'm trying to avoid more "I told you so's" from Tonya. Because I know it's bound to happen. But that's not the only reason. It's literally busy in here and it's all hands-on deck, even with the new help. People are shuttling from table to table behind us and I feel horrible for sitting here talking when I could be lending a hand.

"Sorry," Tonya squeaks. "Sometimes it's hard to remember that you own this place and run an actual business whenever I want to chat."

"It's okay," I laugh. "Now that we have more people working, I'll be able to take days off and we can spend them girl chatting all you want." It'll be a nice little break. I'm constantly working seven days a week.

"It's about time and don't think I won't take you up on any lunch dates."

"I know you will." I wave bye and head back toward the bar, weaving through people delivering food and standing around tables. Dylan goes in the opposite direction to see if his tables need anything. Just like that, he's back in work mode.

Carlos is grinning when I stop by to grab the latest drink order. "What?" I ask. The question coming out harsher than I intended.

"Oh, nothing," he smirks. "I guess you and him are the real deal, huh."

"What makes you say that?" I practically insinuated it earlier.

"Maybe the fact that you had your arms linked together. Or that you were late coming into work. You know the usual things you never do, but all of a sudden are doing." He has a point but I refuse to let him know that.

"Is it so bad? Do you not want me to be happy?"

"No, it's not that," he shakes his head. "I just worry about what's going to happen whenever he moves back home. Are you going to be able to handle that?"

This is why he's one of my best friends. Above all else, no matter how much he doesn't agree with the decision that I make, he has my back. And always has my best interests at heart. And yeah, I'm wondering if I'm going to be able to handle it. I'm allowing myself to get close to him, which is something I've never done. I told him things that I've never told anybody and we've only technically been together one day.

"I don't know." I shrug grabbing the glasses off the bar and setting them on the tray. "We will have to cross that bridge when we get there. Either we'll make the long-distance thing work, he'll stay here, or..."

"You better not finish that or with an 'I'm going to move wherever he is'. That is out of the question." Carlos crosses his arms over his chest. "How am I supposed to handle this bar all by myself? Without you here to boss me around."

"Funny thing, actually," I lean closer. "I have something I want to talk to you about."

He sets the last drink on the tray. "I don't know if I

want to know. But I guess I won't have a choice. Talk about it after work?"

"Yep, I need to get these drinks to the table before the group of sorority girls gets antsy."

"Good luck," he calls out as I'm turning.

"Thanks, I'm going to need it." They are the bubbly type, and I only have space in my life for one person like that. Mostly because Lisa didn't give me much of a choice. I rush to the table, give them their drinks, and take their order for appetizers. There's one thing about these girls they don't play around. The appetizer order is huge, and I have a feeling their food order will be just as big. Not to mention, they'll be keeping this table until close at the rate they're going.

The night continues like this. A steady ebb and flow of people coming in and out. The line outside is slowly shrinking and finally, everyone who wants into Out of the Ashes is inside. Most of those with work tomorrow, or families, have gone on home. Now we're left with not necessarily a rowdy bunch. But they're not quiet either. Hopefully, it doesn't turn into a one of those nights again.

Anytime I have a moment to see what Dylan's doing, he is looking in my direction. Before he would look away and keep his distance. Now he lets me know I'm on his mind by holding my gaze. Between the stolen glances and the barely there touches, I almost want to call off the meeting up with Carlos after work. But it's one we need to have.

Too bad even that fact doesn't change my thought process. The only thing I can think about is Dylan. In my bed, beneath me or on top. It doesn't matter. Though I am wondering what would happen if he took complete control. I need to work on my patients if I ever want to find out.

From across the bar, Carlos nods his head in the direction of a table on the other side of the room. A few guys are raising their voices at each other, and it's a flashback to the night Dylan came into the bar for the first time. For a split second, I consider moving to intervene. I don't have to, though. Dylan is already at their table. I'm not sure what he's telling them. But they get their act together fairly quick.

Maybe he wasn't wrong when he said I needed him to defuse situations And he did it beautifully. There weren't any fists thrown, and my customers didn't end up being shoved out the door. It's a win-win on all sides.

I notice Carlos watching the interaction and I've beam with pride when he sees me watching him. "You know he's not half bad. He talked them down pretty quickly."

"Let's just say he's used to it." I for sure don't want to get into why that is. Besides, it's not my story to tell. It's his if he ever decides to. It all goes back to when he was a kid and the circle he used to hang out with. Carlos doesn't know them and he doesn't know the dynamic. Back then, these kids were dumb. Dylan was the one who had to set them right and make sure they didn't do anything stupid. Well, him and Marshall. It was usually Jake or Randall. They were the hotheads of the group and tended to get into more trouble than most other kids. And, well, Cami, because she liked to egg things on. Though Tonya usually put out those fires.

"It makes sense. Knight is a good addition to the team. Not factoring in how I feel about you and him doing whatever you're doing."

"I agree, but I don't care what you think about what we're doing. I love you Carlos, but that part is off limits unless I come to you for advice. Understand?" I hate having to put this barrier up with him. It sucks, but it's the only way he's going to lay off.

He puts his hands up in surrender. "I just hope you don't have to come to me for that talk." Yeah, buddy. Me too.

* * *

The bar is finally closed and everyone is helping with nightly clean up duties. I fully intend on staying later than normal since I came in over halfway through the day. The new folks look like they have everything under control with Lisa and Dylan directing them.

How did that happen? It took months for me to trust Lisa with leading anything. Dylan is here less than a few weeks and I'm already treating him the same as her. I'm not sure if it's because I've known him since he was little, or because he's gotten under my skin. But I know when he does leave, I won't be the only one with a hole to fill. The essence of the bar will need it too. He's engrained himself here in such a short amount of time.

The meeting with Carlos needs to happen, though. I pass Lisa on the way to the bar, "y'all got this?"

"Yep." She nods her head toward Dylan, expecting me to go toward him. Shaking my head I keep going in my original direction, toward Carlos.

"You ready for that meeting?" My knuckles tap on the bar. It's loud, but can't be heard over the music still playing through the speakers. Even though we're closed, the shutdown process goes so much faster when music is involved. I don't know what it is, but it's magical.

"Sure thing." He tosses his towel on top of the bar. He pauses on his way from behind it to talk to one of the new bartenders. Most likely giving her things she needs to check off her list. She nods and he continues in my direction. "Here? Or in the office?"

"Office." I lead us down the hallway and close the door once we're both inside. "How do you feel about a raise?"

"It depends," he follows me to the desk and sits in one of the two chairs in front of it. I take the one opposite him. I may be coming at this from a professional standpoint, but I'm still his friend. There's no need for me to use the desk as a separation for us. "Does this raise mean more responsibility?"

I pull my hands over my chest, covering my heart as if he's wounded me. "Wow, that hurts."

"It's true, though." He smirks. "What else do you want me to do around here?"

He's not wrong. He does so much for me. Fills in when I can't be here and knows pretty much all the business stuff to help run it. Stella knows some things but she works on the bigger picture. He knows the day to day, how to make this place function no matter what. "It's not so much what else you can do. It's more so giving you the title you deserve. I want you to be an assistant manager, or co-manager. Whatever wording you like."

"What does that mean for me as a bartender? I know I'm surly sometimes, but I do honestly love taking care of drinks for people."

"You can still do that if you want," I rush out. "I mean hell, I was bar owner, bartender, and waitstaff all by myself before you and Lisa came along." He doesn't answer right away, and that makes me nervous. "You can have time to think about it. It's not a lot of extra work, mostly everything you do now, and you'll get a say in the hiring. I'm obviously not that great at choosing people, since most of them leave after a few months."

"Can I also bring some other positions we may need to you? There are some things that will help take some of the weight off everyone if they had their own positions." Now it's his turn to wait for an answer from me.

"Absolutely. We're growing faster than I thought possible and there are a lot of pain points in the process."

"Great," he smiles and stands. He doesn't head for the door like I think he's going to. Instead, he walks behind my desk and grabs a bottle of whiskey. "Now, I'm not trying to sound like an ass, but this promotion doesn't haven't anything to do with Dylan does it?" He pours the liquid into two solo cups. I keep some back here just in case.

I shake my head. "No, I've been wanting to do this for a while. I was only worried you'd bail on me."

"What changed your mind?" He hands me a glass.

"Seeing how you handled today told me everything I needed to know." I take a drink and welcome the warm burn as I swallow. At the mention of his name, I can't help but wonder if he's still here.

I hear a shuffle outside the door, but it could be anyone. The bathrooms are in the same hallway. Ignoring it I put my attention back on Carlos. We have business to take care of. Who knows, maybe one day I'll see if he wants to be my partner. "Want to hash out some of the details while we're here?"

20

dylan

ANGIE HAS BEEN HOLED up in her office for almost thirty minutes. Her and Carlos are talking about business stuff, I'm sure, but it doesn't stop the insecurity running through me. I finally got what I want. What if *he* is into her? That could be why he's so pissed I'm around.

He hasn't liked me since that first night I came in here. I thought after his little speech to me earlier; we were okay. I know most people would think I'm a little young for her. It doesn't matter, though. Not to me. Hopefully not to her either. The one thing I *do* know is I want to spend more time with her outside of work.

I'm grateful I get to see her, but I want more. She does, too. I can feel that, especially after she put her arm through mine in a room full of people. The way this town talks, everyone will know we are an item. I'm ready for whatever comes with the small town gossip. She should be, but she's also never had the gossip mill around her. At least, not that I can recall.

A part of me wants to knock on the door, interrupt whatever it is they are discussing. Anything to assuage the jealousy inside me. My hand is raised to do just that, but I can't. If she thinks I'm clingy, it will ruin everything.

I lower my hand and walk back down the hallway. If she wants to see me when she's done, she can call me. Right now, I need to get home and make sure everything is okay with Mom.

My car is within feet when my phone buzzes with a message. My heart skips a beat, hoping it's Angie, but the display shows its Mom.

MOM

Can you grab me a shake on your way home?

DYLAN

Why aren't you in bed?

MOM

I got wrapped up in this show and I can't sleep.

DYLAN

Okay. What kind?

MOM

Chocolate, please.

I wonder what she's watching that has her not sleeping. It has to be a good one. She usually falls asleep within minutes of any movie. I open my car door and glance back at the bar. Angie still hasn't come out. Oh well. I'll hear from her later, or in the morning.

The streets are empty and quiet as I make my way through town. Almost all of the restaurants are closed and

I'm not exactly sure where my mom expects me to get a chocolate shake at one o'clock in the morning. But I will find a place even if it means I have to drive to a bigger town or city to do it. Her happiness is all that matters to me. Well, not all that matters because there's also Angie. But right now, if I can find this one thing to cure her sweet tooth, I'll do it. Especially after everything she's done for me.

Finally, I find a place on the edge of town close to the highway. It looks vacant, but there's a car in the parking lot, so I'm assuming somebody is working. I pull up to the speaker in the drive thru and wait for the intercom to crackle with a voice.

"Hi, what can I get you tonight?"

"Uh, yeah, can I get two medium chocolate shakes?"

"Will, that'd be it?"

"Yes, thank you." Wow, that guy is all business. It might be the fastest I've ever had an order taken anywhere.

I pull around to the window and hand over my card to the guy working the drive thru. He looks familiar, but I can't quite place him. "Dylan is that you?"

"Yes. Hi, um..."

"Blake, remember from school?"

"Yes, Blake." I snap my fingers. Great, one of my normal tormentors. Which never made sense back then because we were on the same team together. He was all buddy-buddy with Jake, but apparently, I was scum beneath his feet because he had nothing to do with me. Even when I was hanging out with Jake and Marshall, he acted as if I didn't exist. But I wasn't the only one he treated that way. Randall was too. I don't know if it's because both of us come from broken homes. Or because we didn't have the money that some of our friends had. I only know at that age, it sucked.

"Yeah, how have you been?" Don't think it doesn't fill me with glee that he is working at a drive thru in the middle of the night. Does that make me a bad person? Maybe. But I also know that Karma is a bitch, and it actually pays off sometimes.

"Oh, I'm good. Just you know, working." He hands me my card. "I heard you were back in town."

"Yeah. I've been back for a few weeks, helping my mom out." I put my card back in my wallet, hoping this whole interaction ends quickly.

"That's good. That's good." He's nodding as if he's agreeing to something I don't know about. Small talk is the absolute worst. A few seconds later he hands over the chocolate shakes. Apparently, there is someone else working because he hasn't left his spot. "'Well, we'll have to hang out sometime while you're in town."

The desperation on his face almost makes me pity him. But I'm not that big of an asshole. Well, not completely, but maybe he has changed. It seems everyone in my group has and maybe I should give him the benefit of the doubt. "Absolutely. I'm working over at Out of the Ashes right now. So maybe I'll see you around."

"Definitely," he waves before closing the window and I pull away. This is probably the weirdest thing that's happened to me since I've been back in town. And I hope like hell I'm not making the wrong choice hanging out with Blake after all this time.

Mom's sitting on the couch, in darkness when I get home. The only sign of lights are the images flashing across the TV screen. There are men and women in colorful dresses and suits dancing across the screen. It looks like it's from an earlier time period. But it's modernized if that makes sense. And is that an instrumental Taylor Swift song?

What in the world is she watching? "Hey Mom, I'm here with your shake."

I'm not sure why I announced myself. I'm sure she heard the door open. "Oh, thank you, sweetheart. Do you want to watch this with me?"

"What is it?" I hand her the shake and sit down on the sofa next to her.

"It's a show called *Bridgerton*, I think it's based on books. But I'm really loving this. It's a love story, and it takes place in the 1800s. It's really, really good. I think it's been out for a bit, but you know how rarely I get to watch anything."

I laugh. Of course, she would like a show based on a book. Not that there's anything wrong with that. It's just I haven't seen her read in forever. "No, I think I'm gonna go lay down. It was a busy night at work. And then I ran into Blake when I was getting your shake."

"Isn't that the kid that used to give you hell in high school?" She scrunches up her nose in disgust.

"Yep, that would be the one. He wants to get together while I'm in town."

"Are you going to? Because he honestly hasn't changed that much. From what I hear, he gives everybody a hard time and calls into work every chance he can."

"Then probably not." Wow. Okay, so he hasn't exactly changed since back then. Good to know. I guess it's a good thing we didn't exchange numbers or anything, otherwise he'd have a way to get ahold of me.

I grab onto the side of the couch to stand up but my mom holds my arm. She pauses the show and turns toward me. Her casted foot hanging over the edge of the couch. "So, are you and Angie a thing?"

"Maybe. Why?" She's not usually a busy body when it

comes to my personal life. So, I'm wondering what her angle is.

"Oh, just wondering. After the interaction this morning, I kind of hoped maybe something would work out between y'all." She pauses for a moment, and I wonder if she's going to say anything else. "If you have a girlfriend, maybe you won't leave."

Ah, so that's her angle. "Yes, we're seeing each other." I sigh because she's not going to like the next part. "But that doesn't change the fact that I still have a life to go home to."

"Are you sure about that? Because I got a call from your boss, asking you to call him back. Something about layoffs at the job." I don't miss her smug expression. She's never had a problem with me living so far away before. What's changed since then?

Why the hell would he call her? I wasn't even aware he had her number. And then I remember the employment form and she's my emergency contact. Now it makes sense. "That was always a possibility. Even before I came home to help you out, but I have an application in at a couple of other shops in town. I'm just waiting to see if I hear from one." Do I want to leave? Not really. Not now anyway. And seeing my group of friends happy, healthy and in great relationships that don't cause each other harm makes me want to stay. But it's hard when, even when I was here, they didn't treat me like I was a part of the group.

"What if you don't?"

"Well, I guess I'll see what happens." It's all I can do.

"At least you have a job right now. And there is, in fact, an auto shop here in Asheville. I know Johnny would love some additional help." That's the second time someone has mentioned working with Johnny today. It might be something worth looking into if I need to. "Just think about it, Son."

"I will, Mom." I lean over and kiss her on the forehead. "I think I'm gonna go to bed now."

"Goodnight, sweetheart." I'm halfway down the hallway to my room when she calls out. "You forgot your phone. There's a message on it from Angie."

That stops me in my tracks. I turn around and rush back to the living room. Mom is wearing a goofy grin on her face. "What does it say?"

Mom only reaches for her walker and stands. "I'll just go watch this in my room. I'll see you in the morning." She turns off the TV, leaving me in total darkness.

I swipe open my phone and click on the text box.

ANGIE

Are you awake?

DYLAN

Yeah what's up?

Did I text too fast? She's going to think I've been here stalking my phone, waiting to hear from her. But for once I wasn't. I was hanging out with my mom and going to bed.

ANGIE

Can I come over?

DYLAN

Sure. My mom just went to bed, but I think she made herself scarce on purpose.

ANGIE

See you in a few.

This is the part I never experienced as a teenager. The giddy feeling of a girl coming to see me. It's ten times better now. Even though I feel weird about Mom being just a few rooms down. There's one thing for certain, if by some miracle I end up staying here, I'm going to have to get my own place.

21

angie

THE LIGHT in the living room is on when I pull up to Dylan's house. Well, his mom's place, I guess. It should make me feel weird as a woman in my thirties pulling up to see my guy at his mom's house. These are unusual circumstances, though.

ANGIE

I'm here.

DYLAN

The doors unlocked.

This whole thing feels like we're doing something wrong. Like both of us are teetering on this precipice, and if we go too far on one side, we'll fall. One broken heart over the other. That doesn't matter to me right now, though. I want to spend whatever time I have with him. If there's one thing Carlos got right, it's that Dylan will eventually leave.

Stepping out of the car, I close the door gently behind

me. I don't want to wake up the entire neighborhood. It takes me less than a minute to get to the front door. Turning the knob, I push open the door. I'm not sure what to expect. It's definitely not two wine glasses sitting on the old coffee table, or what looks like a romance movie of some sort playing on the TV.

Dylan stands and meets me as I close the door. "Hey," he wraps his arms around me. "I didn't think I was going to see you until tomorrow."

"Yeah, sorry about that."

"I was waiting around, but figured whatever you and Carlos were talking about was important." His voice is strained. Is that a hint of jealousy? That can't be right. He has to know Carlos and I have zero interest in each other.

"Yeah, I actually just asked him to my assistant manager. It'll take some of the workload off of me."

"That means we'll get some actual time together without you rushing off to the bar."

"I said some," I laugh. "There's still a lot I have on my plate. And it'll be worse once you leave."

He leads me to the couch and motions for me to sit down. "Hey, some is better than none."

"So, what's all this?"

All I saw were the wine glasses when I came in. I didn't know there were also cheese slices, crackers, and pickles. It's like a tiny charcuterie board on a paper plate just for us. It's not anything grand, but it's perfect and sweet.

"I didn't want you to come over and me not have anything prepared. I actually planned on us trying to do a picnic and grabbed some stuff when I went to the grocery store. Now, I'm using it, just earlier than I thought."

"I love it. What are we watching?" I want to ask him if

this is going to be long term. I need to know, but for now, I'll play the whole thing by ear.

"It's some show my mom was binging when I got home. I figured we could give it a try. Unless you want to talk or something."

"No, this is fine." I honestly don't remember the last time I watched anything.

"Good deal."

He leans forward pouring us both a glass of wine and hands me one. I lean back and snuggle into him while he presses play. I don't even know how long I'll stay awake but this...this feels nice. Being appreciated like this after a long day's work is something I've never experienced or allowed myself to. If it wasn't the bar, I didn't let myself enjoy it.

For the first time in years, I feel like I deserve this. I just never thought it would be with *him*. Or that he'd be more mature than most of the men my age. Things seem to be on the upswing, and I'm here for it.

* * *

Is that bacon? The smell wakes me up and I realize I'm no longer on the couch. Dylan is lightly snoring behind me. I don't even remember coming to his bed last night. Maybe he carried me. Lifting the blankets, I notice I'm still wearing my clothes from last night. I slide off the bed and open the door. I don't want to wake him.

My steps are silent as I make my way down the hall. Let's just say I've had lots of practice being quiet. Thank you for days of sneaking out of the house in high school. I only got caught once, and learned to be more careful in the future.

Mrs. Knight is standing at the stove when I get to the

kitchen. One foot planted firmly on the ground, and the leg she has a cast on is resting on the walker. A radio playing old rock on the counter fills the silence. It's not loud enough to be heard from Dylan's room, just loud enough for her to bop her head to as she adds bacon to a frying pan.

"Do you need any help?"

She jumps and grabs on the walker for balance. "You scared me, Angie."

This should be awkward. I'm not even a serious girl-friend and I just walked out of her son's room in the same clothes I was wearing yesterday. But it's not. I spent so much time here in my teens, and when I was in college, watching Dylan while she was at work, that it feels almost like a second home.

"Sorry," I wince. "I'll try to be louder."

"It's okay. Do you know how to fry eggs?"

Do I know how to? Yes. Am I any good at it? That's debatable.

"Sure. Where is the pan?"

"Down there in the cabinet. I only want one, but make a few for Dylan and yourself. We should be done at about the same time."

"Yes ma'am."

We work in a companionable silence for a few moments. I've always admired this woman. She managed to work two jobs, raise a son, and still somehow show up for his games when they weren't too far. If there's ever a day I become a parent, I want to be like her. Minus the two jobs. Though running the bar feels like three or four jobs some days.

"So, you and Dylan are hitting it off I take it?"

"Um, yes?"

"You don't sound so sure about that. You know he's had

a crush on you for as long as I can remember. I thought maybe one day when you were both grown, he might get up the nerve to ask you out."

"I'm sure, but I know he isn't here to stay. When he leaves, I can't just uproot my life and go with him. I have the bar to run." I flip the eggs and think on the last part of the sentence. "The age difference doesn't bother you?"

She laughs. It's not quite the reaction I expected. "Not in the slightest. Dylan's dad was quite a few years older than me when we met, before he broke things off with me when Dylan was born. Age has never bothered me."

Another reason to admire her. She lays out the facts, and she doesn't sound bitter about Dylan's dad taking off. That's not exactly how most women would feel.

"That's good to know."

"Will you try the long-distance thing if he leaves?"

"Maybe. We aren't exactly doing the labels thing, but we're seeing where this goes between us."

Wait a minute, she said if, not when. Does she know something I don't? I'm about to ask her, but I hear Dylan's footsteps come down the hall.

"Mom, what are you doing cooking breakfast?" He rushes to the stover and tries to pull the tongs out of her hand. But she bats him away.

"I can get around. I'm even using this stupid walker."

"I know, but do you have the strength for it?"

"Look here, Son. I managed to get things done while you've been living in another state for years. I'm perfectly capable of doing things now. You worry too much."

"Well sorry for making sure your foot heals correctly." He crosses his arms over his chest then walks over to where I'm standing and plants a quick peck on my cheek.

"It's heeling just fine." Mrs. Knight pulls the last of the

bacon out of the pan as I slide the last egg onto a plate. "Now, let's eat. Y'all can fill me in on how things are going at the bar. I'm going stir crazy in this house and need something to think about."

"I bet. Your son should take you out for lunch, or dinner, instead of trying to confine you in his version of bubble wrap."

"I knew I liked you," she smiles.

Dylan grabs the plates and sets them on the small table in the center of the kitchen. He mouths "traitor" in my direction before holding the chair out of his mom to sit down. She rests her leg on the seat area of the walker and we all dig into our breakfast.

It's a change of pace for how breakfast was at my parents' growing up. That was absolute chaos. My brother running around the house looking for sports gear or his car keys. Mom badgering me about my assignments. I wonder if this is how it's always been for these two. The peek into their lives is nice. It helps see how they interact now as opposed to when he was a kid.

Once we're finished with breakfast, his mom goes to the living room. He picks up the dishes and carries them to the sink. The faucet runs as he fills the sink with water. Watching him wash dishes might be the sexiest thing I've ever seen. The way his forearm flexes with each scrub, it just does something for me. Too bad I don't have time right now. I need to get changed and head to work.

I wrap my arms around his waist. "I wish I could stay and help you out, but I have some things I need to do. You can always come do dishes at my house, though."

He turns and flings soap at me. "And why is that?"

"I think you know."

"So, doing dishes. A major turn on. I'll have to keep that

in my back pocket." He leans down and presses his lips to mine. Pulling away, he tips my chin up. "See you later?"

"Absolutely." I head for the front door before I have second thoughts and stay with him. I really need to keep some sort of boundary between him and work. Kinda hard since he's one of my employees, but we'll make it work.

22

dylan

ANGIE HAS COME over the past few mornings. I think breakfast with my mom is her new favorite thing. Not that I'm complaining. Having my two favorite people in the same room has been amazing. They get along like they've been friends for years. In ways I guess they have. At least since I was a kid. Though the relationship has changed through time. It went from her paying a teenager to take care of her stubborn kid, to that of neighbors, and now... something more. Hopefully, anyway. If there's anything that can make me stay in this town, it's her.

"Where's Angie?" Mom is coming from her room to the living room. She's taking advantage of sleeping in. She deserves it.

"I'm not sure."

"I hope I didn't run her off."

"You didn't. She may have some things to do before the bar opens."

"Yeah, she does take pride in that place. It's much nicer now than when her uncle owned it. A better crowd, too."

It's hard not to hear the judgment in her voice. But I get it. It's where she met my dad. I've never met him. I spent my entire childhood wondering if he'd come looking for me. If he'd want anything to do with me. I'm in my twenties now. He obviously didn't.

"Yeah, it's the place to be these days." I stand and give mom a quick hug. "I'm going for a run. If Angie stops by, let her know I'll see her soon."

"Will do." Mom takes my place and turns on the TV. She's watching that show again. How many times has she seen it? I think it may be her new obsession.

I grab my ear buds off the table by the door and shove my phone in my pocket. I need to think. Not just about why Angie didn't show up this morning. But also, the call I need to make soon. I'm sure my boss is waiting for me to return his call. I already know what he's going to say. I've been refreshing my email more than normal as well. None of the other jobs I applied for have contacted me. Maybe this is a sign.

My feet hit the pavement, and I run on the sidewalk in front of the house this time instead of in the alley. People know I'm back in town, there's no use trying to hide it.

The ear buds play a steady beat. Rock pouring through the tiny speakers. My thoughts are all over the place and it takes me a few moments to realize there's a car driving alongside me. And it's honking. Slowing my jog, I head to the curb. Angie is waiting and grinning from ear to ear.

"Took you long enough."

"Sorry, I guess I was in my own world."

"Obviously," she laughs.

"How long were you driving alongside me?"

"Not too long, but long enough to seem like a creeper."

"My bad. Next time I'll run with only one ear bud in."

"That's probably a good idea." She gestures to the empty passenger seat beside her. "Get in?"

I didn't finish my full run, but I'll take any chance on alone time with her. It feels like it comes so infrequently since we've been dating. Some days it feels like she uses other people as a buffer between us, and I crave these moments.

"You were late for breakfast this morning." It comes out as an accusation even if I don't mean for it to. "Mom was asking about you."

"I know. I meant to call, but I didn't have time." She sighs and grips the wheel. "There was a leak in the kitchen and I had to rush up there and figure out what the hell was going on."

Now I feel like an asshole. I finally have what I want. Who I want. Why am I trying to destroy that before we have a real shot at a future together? It feels like high school all over again. Like know matter what I do, I'll be the least important person. Which isn't fair to her. She had an actual emergency with her business. Maybe it's a combination of that and most likely being laid off. It's almost too much to handle.

"Did you get it figured out?"

"Yeah. The plumber is on his way. We'll have to close the bar for the day which sucks. But that means we get all day together."

Those five words mean everything to me and manage to alter my mood. Enough to let me worry about everything else another time. "What do you have in mind?"

"First, we need to get you changed. You're sweaty and gross."

"I'm not sure what you mean." I scoot closer to her and throw my arms around her. "I'm not gross at all."

"Stop, Dylan," she giggles. Actually, giggles like a school girl. I haven't heard her do that since I used to spy on her talking to her friends when I was a kid. "I'm going to drop you off. Get ready and be at my house in an hour."

"Isn't it supposed to be my job to wow you?"

"You have been. Now it's my turn."

She puts the car in drive and turns around in someone's driveway. We're at my house in minutes. "One hour. Don't forget."

I lean over to give her a kiss, but she backs up. "I don't think so mister. Not until you're cleaned up."

"Fine, fine. I'll see you in a bit. Do I need to bring anything?"

"Nope. Just you." She surprises me and gives me a quick peck on my cheek before pushing me toward the door. "Now hurry."

I can't help but wonder what exactly she has planned. Was she just being coy and hinting at something more intimate? Or does she actually have a day planned for us? One that she pulled out of thin air after an unexpected snafu at the bar. It's odd, but I'm not going to second guess it. Her showing up is exactly what I needed to put my fears to rest.

* * *

The last thing I expect to see when I pull up to Angie's is her wearing jeans, boots and a tank top. Now I wish I knew what she has planned. I look down at my clothes wondering if I'm dressed appropriately. I guess I'll find out soon enough. I step out of the car and close the door. "I like this look."

She pauses in front of her door and spins. "You think?"

"Absolutely."

It'd be a hell of a lot sexier if she lost the jeans. Once I'm in front of her I wrap my arms around her waist, lifting her off the ground. Her arms go around my neck, and my mouth crashes into hers. The kiss is long and deep. My tongue exploring while one of my hands reaches behind her for the door knob. She breaks the kiss and smacks my hand away.

"I don't think so. At least, not right now. I have things planned."

"Me bending you over your bed isn't on the list? I'm hurt."

"Shut up." She starts walks down the driveway and I'm expecting her to keep going to my car, but she stops. "Oh yeah, and I'm driving."

"Why?"

"Because your day is about to be full of surprises."

If there's anything I've learned from when I was younger and in the past few weeks, it's not to argue with her. Though that is how I got my job. Maybe I should argue more. I walk to the passenger side of her car and get in. This feels weird. I don't even remember the last time I've been on this side of a car.

"Can I ask where we're going?"

"You can ask all you want, but I'm not telling."

She puts the key in the ignition and starts the car. I hope like hell wherever she's taking us is private. It's a full day off with just us, and I'd like to keep it that way.

* * *

Wait. I know where this road is going. I haven't been this way since high school. I'm curious why she chose here of all places to spend the day. My clothes are definitely not appropriate, if we're doing what I think we are. Especially the shoes. Zero grip on these Vans.

Angie pulls onto the long driveway leading to her brother's ranch. All the hot summer days were almost unbearable working the field, cattle, and horses, but it was worth it. It's what bought my first car. This place holds a lot of great memories for me.

Colton is already standing in the small parking area in front of his house. The car slows and we get it out once she puts it in park. He doesn't even give us a chance to close the doors and he's at Angie's side. "It's been too long, lil sis." He wraps her in a bear hug.

"Well, I've been busy."

"How did you manage to get today off?"

"There was a leak in the kitchen. I decided to close the bar for the day while it gets fixed. No sense in rushing to go in and making the plumber hurry."

"Won't you lose business?"

"It'll be okay. We're slow during the week."

He finally catches sight of me. "Well, look who blew into town."

I walk around the car and shake his hand. "It's good to see you, man."

"Why haven't you come by to say hi?" He sounds hurt, and I feel bad. This family has done nothing but look out for me. My reasons for seeking out Angie were purely for my own benefit. But I obviously suck and showing up for the others the same way they have for me.

"Sorry, I've been working almost every day at the bar."

"Oh yeah, what does my sister have you doing?"

"Wait staff mostly, but I also take care of any skirmishes that might arise."

"Sounds like a good job for you." He opens his arms wide taking in the whole ranch. "If you ever want to work with me again, you're more than welcome."

"I'm good at the bar for now."

"Ah," he sighs. Does he know I'm leaving? I don't want him to think his sister means nothing to me. Hell, he knew I was working to get a car to take his sister out. It's good knowing he doesn't see anything odd with us dating. Their parents may have something else to say about that. He turns toward the barns. "I saddled up two of the calmest horses we have. I know you haven't ridden in a while, Ang. And I doubt you've ridden since you worked here." He points at me.

He's not wrong. "Do you have any boots I can borrow? Your sister didn't tell me what she had planned for the day."

"Yeah, let me go grab some. Those shoes definitely won't cut it. Not when it's been so long since you've been on a horse."

"Thanks."

Colton goes inside and I turn toward the woman who dragged me out here. "Surprise," she waves her hands in the air.

"Why riding?"

"I figured we could get lost for a while. I even packed a lunch for us."

I'm impressed. I can't help but wonder what it is. "What do you mean by get lost?"

23

angie

I REMEMBER NOW why I have a love hate relationship with riding. It's exhilarating and painful at the same time. At least I remembered to wear jeans. I can't even imagine how bad my legs would be chafing if I wore shorts. "How's this for our impromptu picnic?"

Dylan turns his head from side to side, taking in the area. "It's perfect."

He lifts one leg up and over the horse. As if he's been riding this entire time. I'm jealous of how easily he picked it back up. Not surprising. He's always been good at things. It takes almost no effort on his part, in anything he puts his mind to. One of the many things I admire about him.

He's at my side before I have a chance to try and climb my way off the horse. He places his hands on my waist and lifts me off the horse like it's nothing. "I'm capable of getting off without you."

"Huh," he snorts. "I'd like to revisit that topic later and see just how many times I can get you off."

That should sound douchey. Coming from any other guy's mouth, it would be. But him...he can pull it off, and I'm interested in the answer as well. "How about we eat first?"

"I was thinking the same thing."

His hand trails over the button of my jeans, but I back away. "Food Dylan. We need to eat food first. After that, we'll see what happens."

I grab the bag off the saddle and Dylan leads the horses to a nearby tree. He wraps the reins loosely around it. I pick a shaded area further away to lay down the blanket and set out the food. I love my brother's horses, but I don't want them begging me for food.

Our little picnic is laid out when Dylan joins me. He sits down next to me and pulls me close. "I've missed riding. I didn't realize how much until today. I may take your brother up on his offer."

"As long as you don't hurt yourself. I still need you at the bar." I pause for a second. "Until you leave anyway."

Already those words are a stab to the gut. I don't want him to leave. He's wormed his way under my skin, and it's going to be hard as hell to let him go.

"About that...I might not be leaving. At least, not for long."

"Really? Why?"

"Before I came down here, the shop I worked at was laying people off. With the chain shops coming up in the area, it's getting harder and harder for him to compete. It's family run, and I'm not family."

"Damn, that sucks. I'm sorry."

That's what I say out loud. On the inside, I'm celebrating. Now that I've had him in my life, regardless of how short the time, I can't imagine him being gone. This is it. The moment he decides to stay.

"Yeah. It's not how I planned for things to happen, but what can you do?"

"Are you going to stay on at the bar?"

"That's the idea. At least for now. I have a few applications in at other shops back home."

Now the bubble has burst. He still has every intention of going back. Of leaving Asheville, possibly for good. "Well," I clear my throat, trying to hide any emotion. I don't want him to know just how much I'm falling for him. "You have a job as long as you need one."

He picks up one of the sandwiches I made and takes a bite. "And if I need one long term?"

Is he saying what I think he is? This conversation is a ping pong match. Stay or go. He has no idea what he wants. That terrifies me. He's the only thing I've wanted aside from the bar. Hell, I've never brought any guy I casually dated out here. Though, he knows the ranch about as well as I do. But I wouldn't bring him around family if I didn't think it could go somewhere.

I pull the sandwich out of his hand, set it down on the bag, and climb over him. "I told you," I bend down and kiss the side of his neck. "You have a job as long as you need."

He leans back against the tree and groans. "And what about you? Do I have you regardless of what happens?"

Does he? I don't know. As long as he's here...yes. But if he leaves, I'm not so sure. I don't know if my heart can handle a long-distance relationship. If I'm in, I'm all in. That's just not possible if he's living in a different state.

Instead of answering, I run my hands over his chest, kissing right under his jaw. Waiting to see if I'm properly distracting him from a question I'm not ready to answer.

My fingers trailing over the soft cotton until I get to the hem. I yank it up, and he sits up, allowing me to pull it over his head. He doesn't let me do much else, though.

One arm goes around my waist and before I can blink, my back is against the blanket and his centered between my legs. This. This is what I wanted from him the first time we had sex. His fingers work the button of my jeans and within seconds they are undone. This isn't going to be slow and sweet. No, he needs to let out frustration. So, do I.

Besides the bar, he's the only person that makes me feel alive. And right now, I'll let him take whatever he needs. As much as I like to control things, I need to leave it behind this once. Let him take the lead.

His lips crash into mine and I reach for the bag I packed. I'm nothing if not prepared. I threw a few condoms in here this morning just in case. I'm glad my instincts were right.

He pulls back, "what are you doing?"

"Looking for the condoms I stashed."

"Were you going to seduce me?"

"No. I just figured the opportunity might arise."

"Hmm." No words. Just a noncommittal syllable. He grabs the bag and moves things around until he pulls out a square foil packet. The bag lands who knows where, but right now I really don't care. He opens the condom with his teeth and it may be the hottest thing I've ever seen. I've read about this in books and seen it in movies. It's much better witnessing it in person.

I push his jeans and boxers down just far enough for his cock to spring free. He leans back to pull my boots off, then my jeans follow. It's a little unfair that I'm half naked and he's not. I'm not complaining, though. Being out in the open like this is exhilarating. Even though it's unlikely, the possibility that someone can come across us is on the edge of my mind, and I don't care. It's also something I've never considered. Being with Dylan makes me reckless. I don't know if that's good, or bad, but I'll take it.

Before I can dwell on that too long, he's inside me. He's not being tender or slow. All I can do is throw my arms around him and hang on. My nails dig into his shoulders as he thrusts harder and faster. All the uncertainty he's feeling, and can sense from me, releasing with every movement.

His arm goes underneath me, arching my back and letting him go deeper. My entire body tenses before letting go. Letting go of any stress or worry I feel about us. I can't help the scream that escapes my lips. He keeps going and before long he comes. Holding onto me as if I have all the answers. Spoiler alert...I don't. I'm just as confused and frustrated as he is.

"Feel better?" It's a question for me as much as it is him.

"Actually," he grins. "Yes, I do. What about you?"

"Yeah, I feel pretty good."

He moves from between my legs, discards the condom, and pulls up his pants. I move to grab my own jeans, but he already has them next to me. Always trying to make things easier for me. "So, are you ready to eat actual food? Since we had dessert first."

"I definitely have an appetite now." I slide my jeans on while he makes the blanket presentable. He sets the sandwiches out again, and pulls two bottles of water out of the bag. Opening one bottle, he hands it to me. "Thanks."

He's sitting across from me and I miss the comfort of having him beside me. "Sorry about that," he motions to the ground where we just fucked our frustrations out of us. "I didn't mean for it to be so—"

"It's okay. You don't have to apologize. I think we both needed it."

Nodding he takes a bite of his sandwich. I feel like he's pulling back into himself and I don't understand why. It could be the age difference, or maybe he's ashamed of what we did. There's no way of knowing unless he opens up and says something. I won't push it. Not right now, anyway. He'll say something when he's ready. I hope. His behavior now is a complete one eighty from a few moments ago.

"What else do you have planned for our day? I have a feeling this wasn't all you had planned."

Nice change of subject. I'll play along, though.

"I figured we could go ride go-carts and then dinner. How does that sound to you?"

He screws up his face. "It sounds like you're hitting the spots I used to frequent as a teen. Don't get me wrong, I loved it then, but I'd rather spend quality time with you."

Huh, I guess I fucked up this day. "So, dinner and back to my place to hang out or watch a movie?"

"I like that idea. We can still do go-carts and arcade games, but not today. We have time." He finishes his sandwich and gathers the trash. "Want to ride for a while longer when you're done eating?"

"Sure." I try like hell to keep my voice chipper.

I'm getting time with him, and that's what I wanted. Hopefully, we can make pick up the vibe I was going for today again. I can't help but feel like there's been a shift. As much as I like him, and want to continue this, I'm beginning to wonder if I'm just not built for relationships. The bar is the longest relationship I've ever had and as much as I love it, maybe I should have been out there trying to date. At least then I would be so damn awkward when it comes to this.

24

dylan

CLOSING the bar for one day made the rest of the week stupid busy. Angie has even called me to come in and help out with the day time shifts. Not that I mind. It's more time with her. Even though she's been acting weird. I thought telling her I was possibly staying in Asheville would make her happy. It seems like she's pulling away. Or maybe I did something wrong.

She seemed like she enjoyed our impromptu tryst in the back area of the ranch, but I could be wrong. It was emotional, not only because I no longer have a job at home. Nothing to return to. It felt like a kick to the teeth to be let go. I know I'm not technically family, even though they treated me like I was. They hired me on after the football team turned their backs on me after my injury. It's like being pushed aside all over again.

"Hey man." I don't even notice who is sitting at the table until they speak. Jake and Marshall are staring at me as if they don't know who I am. "Are you okay?"

Shaking my thoughts loose, I pull out the notepad from my apron. I don't know how Angie and some of the others take orders without writing anything down. I've tried doing it a couple of times and screwed everything up. I don't do that anymore. "Yeah, I'm good. What can I get y'all?"

Jake takes it at face value, but Marshall...he studies me. "Are you sure? You look like someone just kicked your puppy."

"Just thinking."

"Anything we can help with?" Jake takes the menu and looks it over as if he doesn't know every item on it. He comes in a lot with his girlfriend and kids. That's not something I ever imagined I'd see. Jake with kids. "I know I was a dumbass when I was younger, but I like to think I've gotten smarter with age."

Marshall snorts, "barely."

"Maybe," I shrug. "But I don't know if I want to get into it right now."

"We're planning on going to the lake soon. If you're off, you're more than welcome to come." I haven't talked to Jake much since that first night, and I feel shitty about it. Our past may be shitty, but it seems like he's grown up since then. Like he's trying to be better than what his parents raised him to be.

"Yeah, I'd like that."

"We should let you get back to work." Marshall chuckles. "Jake, do you know what you want?"

It feels good seeing them again. And talking to them. Things were so rocky between me and Jake before I left. I didn't realize how much I missed my friend group. Though having Marshall around has always been a nice buffer. He reads the room as well as I do. I take their order and head back to the kitchen.

Angie is standing at the door to the kitchen when I turn the order in. She doesn't notice me at first, and I take her in. When she's here, she's almost always all business. But she has the respect and confidence of her staff. We all know she'll take care of us and help us out if needed. Too bad, what I need help with can't be taken care of here at the bar. I feel like I'm floundering and I don't know how to fix it.

"Hey," I whisper as I pass by her. "You doing okay?"

She startles and I feel bad for not making my presence known. "Yeah, poor Patrick is swamped and I need to hire a few more cooks. He can't manage this on his own."

She's not wrong. The only plus side for him is we don't keep the kitchen open late at night. After the dinner time rush, he gets to go home. I can't imagine handling it all on my own, especially with the popularity the place has gotten.

"I don't have a ton of experience cooking, but I'm great at following directions. I can go back and help him while one of the other folks work my tables."

"You would do that?"

"Absolutely. He's drowning back there." I can't believe she didn't think I would. I am, and have always been, a team player. If one of us flounders all of us do.

"Okay," she throws her arms around me and kisses me on the cheek. "Go help Patrick and I'll split up your tables."

"You got it."

I'm reluctant to let her go. With the way it's been when we're alone, I'm terrified it'll be the last time I hold her. Blame it on young insecurities, or whatever, I can't handle another let down this week. I do let go, though, and turn toward the door.

"Thank you so much. You have no idea how much it means to me."

"Dinner after work?"

"Yes. I think we both need it after this crazy week."

"Deal," I nod. "If it gets insane out here again let me know and I'll help in both places as much as I can."

"If that happens, I'll pull one of the bartenders to work the tables. All that matters right now is getting him the help he needs."

I open the door to the kitchen and offer up a silent prayer. Don't get me wrong I can cook basic things. If Patrick is expecting anything fancy, he'll probably kick me out of the kitchen. Let's see how this goes.

* * *

"You survived." It's the first time Angie has talked to me since I went to the kitchen.

"Barely," I chuckle. "We definitely need to get that man some help. He means business in there."

She leans close to me as if she's sharing a secret. "I'm convinced he's a wizard."

"Whys that?"

"You see how many orders go through there. I don't know how he manages to get them all out without fucking it up."

"He's never had help back there?"

"I did at first, but when the tables got busier, I'd have to divide my attention. Finally, he kicked me out because I was getting in his way."

"I'm surprised he didn't' do the same to me. I'm not exactly quick with cooking."

The man in question comes out of the kitchen. "You did alright. A lot better than she did."

"Hey," Angie scoffs. "I used to cook and wait tables before I brought you on."

"True," he nods. "Also, it's not magic. It's one hundred percent skill."

"Yeah, yeah," Angie waves as he leaves the bar before turning to me. "So, what do you want to do for dinner?"

"What are you in the mood for?"

"I don't know, actually." She taps her finger on her chin. "Definitely no wings or anything we serve here. And I still have a few things to take care of here before we can go."

"I can order some pizzas and have them delivered here."

"You don't have to wait around for me."

"It's not a problem. It'll give me some time to check my email and get in touch with Jake."

"So, you two are building your friendship up again?"

"Baby steps." I grin and pull out my phone to find the closest pizza place. "He invited me to the lake with them."

"Oh." Was that a good word, or bad? I honestly can't tell. "Well, I'm going to get some of the paperwork done while we wait."

"Sounds good." She starts toward the hall and I call out, "Any particular toppings?"

"Nope, I'm good with anything."

After I order the pizza, I glance around the bar area to see if there's anything that need to be done. Everyone is pretty good with cleaning their workspaces, but it doesn't hurt to do another once over. Angie's behavior is really tripping me up. Everything was fine and now it feels so unbalanced. Like I'm one comment away from screwing it all up.

The bar is cleaner than I thought it would be. The bartenders don't play around when it comes to their space. If I had to guess, Carlos is the one who makes sure they clean up. He runs a tight ship, a lot like Angie, and he'll be a hell of a manager. I only hope he doesn't come after me. I know he's not my biggest fan.

There's a knock at the door and I jump. Damn, I forgot how quick pizza gets here when you're right around the corner. Back home, it takes a solid thirty minutes, if not longer, to be delivered. I only hope this place is as good as I remember. Hurrying over to the door, I unlock it. The kid can't be more than seventeen. He's holding out the pizza and shuffling from foot to foot while he waits on me.

"Thanks, man." I grab the pizzas out of his hands and replace it with some cash from my tips tonight. I've always made sure to tip, but after working here, I know exactly how much it matters.

"No problem," he grins after looking at the wad of cash I just gave him. "Don't y'all serve food here?"

"Yeah, but we wanted something different than what is usually on the menu."

"I get it. Too much of the same thing is never a good idea." He waves, "Thanks, sir."

Did...did he just call me sir? Oh no, I am not old enough to be called that. What the hell is going on here? I close and lock the door and notice Angie standing at the edge of the bar, covering her mouth. "What?"

"He just called you sir."

"Yeah, he did," I grunt.

"Doesn't feel so great, does it?"

"Not even a little bit. I'm barely a few years older than him. How the hell did it even cross his mind?"

"I feel the pain," she walks toward me. "The first time some teen called me ma'am, I almost lost it."

"I don't blame you. You are hot as fuck, definitely not old enough to be a ma'am."

She grins and I hope I have the Angie from before the horse riding back. I only wish I knew what I did.

"Well, thanks." She closes the distance between us and

pulls the pizza out of my hands, setting them on the bar. "Want to eat this here? Or go to my place?"

"Eat then go." I shiver at the feel of her fingertips sliding down my chest. We need to talk. Need to figure out what shifted between us, but right now...food and her bed are calling to me. We can figure everything else out later. I did tell her we'd play this, us, by ear. Maybe she's realized she doesn't want a relationship with someone my age. I'll take whatever she's willing to give for as long as I can. Before she decides she wants nothing to do with me, leaving me discarded once again.

25

angie

BOTH DYLAN and I have the day off. Carlos has assured me he has the bar under control. It's hard letting that bit of control go. To let someone else handle my baby while I'm not there. The only thing that could make it better is if I was spending the entire day with Dylan. At least I have this morning. I made things weird after our last full day together. I pulled away when I shouldn't have. He asked me an honest question, and I couldn't give him an answer. I don't know what we would look like if he left Asheville. I do know that I'm attached to him, and I'm not sure I could let him go.

There's a knock on the door. It has to be Dylan. We're planning on taking his mom out to lunch. Get her out of the house and do something nice before he meets his friends at the lake. The same friends I used to babysit. The friends that tossed him aside whenever he didn't go along with whatever they were doing. Jake's grown up a lot, and I hope like hell he realizes how great of a friend Dylan can be.

I also need to remember I can't be the asshole that ditches him when things get tough. Even if the tough thing interrupts my status quo. Giving me something I never thought I wanted.

I grab my purse and open the front door. Only it's not Dylan on my porch. "Mom, what are you doing here?"

"Well, if you'd answer your phone I wouldn't have to show up at your door."

"How did you know I was home?"

"Carlos said you had the day off." She glances inside the house. "Aren't you going to invite me in?"

No is on the tip of my tongue, but if I don't see what she wants, she'll never leave. Maybe if I let her say her piece, I can get her out the door before Dylan gets here. "Sure, come in, Mom."

She doesn't hesitate and barges her way inside. "How have you been? I take it everything at the bar is going well."

"I've been good," I sigh. "Business is picking up again, and the renovations are going well. We're hoping to open up in a month or so."

"Good. Good." She runs a hand along the counter on the way to the living, stopping when she gets to the vase of flowers. Dylan made good on his promise and surprises me with bouquets any chance he can. I have to say they really brighten up the house, and with the amount of time he's been spending here, it looks like someone lives here. "These are beautiful. When did you start getting flowers?"

Crap. I don't know how to answer this. Hell, I don't know how she'll react to me dating someone so much younger than me. "Um," I begin until I'm interrupted by another knock.

Dammit. He would choose now to show up. He's always early, and I should have expected it. I rush to the door and hope like hell he'll be okay with hanging outside for a bit. But when I open it, Mom is at my side. It's not that I'm ashamed of him, I just don't want to have this conversation with my mom while he's here.

"Hey." His smile is wide and he looks so happy. "Are you ready to go? My mom is getting rea—."

His words die on his lips and his eyes widen. "You remember my mom, don't you, Dylan?"

"Hi, Mrs. Donavan." He sticks his hand out to her.

She pushes it away and wraps him in a hug. "Dylan, how have you been? My, you've grown since the last time I saw you."

He's staring at me over her head and mouths help me, but he returns the hug. He's not rude, and I can appreciate that considering he was caught off guard. "Yep. Been eating my *Wheaties*."

Mom leans back and squeezes his arm. "I can tell." She looks between us, no doubt wondering why he's here. "I heard you were working at the bar. Are you here for a work-related thing?"

Dylan looks from me to her. He doesn't say a thing. Only waits to see what I'm going to say. The hurt in his eyes can't be missed, though. I need to finally fill her in on what I've been spending my free time doing.

"No. He's here to spend the day with me, Mom. We're dating."

It takes a moment to sink in before her eyes widen. "Oh. I didn't realize."

Dylan mutters something under his breath, but I don't catch it. Now would be a good time for him to speak up. Except...it's not his place. I should have told her weeks ago. Instead, the only person I've mentioned him to is my brother. Although, I'm surprised she didn't hear about it through the gossip in town. We haven't exactly made it a secret.

"Yeah, for a few weeks now. We don't have a ton of time to go on dates so we take advantage when we both manage to have the day off together."

"I see." After a moment of silence, she touches my arm. "Can I talk to you for a second?"

"I don't really have time right now. We have plans."

I point toward Dylan in case she still doesn't understand who I mean. She gives zero fucks about whatever plans I have because her soft touch turns into a hard grip. "Now, Angie."

Saying no is futile, even if we are in my house. "Can you give us a minute?"

The look on my mom's face says it's going to be much longer than that. He leans against the bar as I walk away. My feet lead me toward the living room, but Mom has a different idea and pulls me into my room. It's not the first time she's done this. There were many times when I was a teen and she did the same thing. I was the more rambunctious type than my brother. He followed every rule, and I...didn't. Not that I was a bad kid, or anything. I simply didn't like being home early. Especially on weekends.

She slams the door behind me and lets go of my arm. "What in the world are you thinking, Angie? You used to babysit that kid. He's way too young for you."

"He's an adult. Just like me. Age is just a number, Mom. As long as we're both consenting, what's the big damn deal?"

"And he works for you," she scolds. "I don't have anything against him, but what will people think?"

"Honestly, they don't think anything. We haven't exactly made us dating a secret. People who come into the bar know. So do our closest friends. Hell, Colton let us go to the ranch and ride horses."

"Your brother knows?" Her screech is loud and high pitched.

I probably shouldn't have mentioned that. But great job on actually keeping your mouth closed big brother. He's kept me out of trouble more times than I can count, but he always ends up ratting me out somehow.

"Look, don't be mad at him. I asked him to keep it quiet."

"That's never stopped him before."

"Because this time he's trying to get me to do something for myself outside of the bar."

"Excuse me? *Do* something. Please tell me he didn't mean that literally."

"He wants me to have something other than Out of the Ashes. Something for myself that has nothing to do with work. Besides, I didn't have to tell him anything. He found out Dylan was back in town a few days after he got here."

"And why didn't you tell me, or your father, about you and Dylan? Are you ashamed of him?"

"Of course not," I scoff. "I'm grown. There's no reason to be ashamed or have to explain myself to you. I'm perfectly capable of making good decisions without you reprimanding me. I'm not a kid anymore. I haven't been for a long time and had to grow up even faster once Uncle Max died and left me the bar. I don't know what you want from me."

I hear my phone ding in the kitchen. There's only two possibilities on who it could be. Carlos with something going wrong at the bar or Dylan. If it's the latter, then he heard at least part of this conversation and jet.

"Look, I don't have time for this right now. Dylan and I have plans. Can we table this for later?"

"I'm not trying to run your life, but it would be nice if your father and I were kept in the loop on what's happening with you. We know you're busy, but this is a big thing. I can't remember the last time you even considered seriously dating someone. Now, you're all of a sudden in a relationship with a kid you babysat in high school?"

"I really wish you'd stop calling him a kid. He's an adult now. Before he came here, he had a job. The only reason he's even in town is because he's been taking care of his mom after she broke her foot."

"So," she says softly. "He isn't planning on staying?"

Why does she have to do this now? Of all the days she could have picked, she decided today was the one she needed to hound me about this. She could have called. Though, she did and I didn't take them.

"Originally, Mom, no. He wasn't going to stay, but the garage he worked at laid him off. He hadn't heard from any other job prospects, so he was heavily considering staying. Why are we even having this discussion?"

"Because I heard rumors, and since you don't answer the phone, I had to show up on your doorstep. This all could have been avoided if you'd called me back. Or even stopped by the house." She wrings her hands together. "It would have been such a shock to me. I also may have come at it differently."

"Mom," I sigh. "There's no reason for you to come at anything from any angle. I *am* grown."

What part of that does she not understand? Actually, I don't have to listen to this. I've always had a great relationship with my family, despite my little stunts as a teen. I open the door and head back to the kitchen. Dylan is nowhere to be seen. I check my phone and there's a message from him.

DYLAN

> It sounds like you're going to be a bit. I'll grab food for my mom and head to the lake early. Maybe I'll see you later tonight.

Great. I hope to hell he didn't hear anything we were talking about. His text message didn't sound angry, but I don't know what's going on in his head. And I won't know until he's done hanging out with his friends.

Mom comes up behind me and lays a hand on my shoulder. "I'm sorry, sweetie."

"Don't, Mom," I shake my head and shrug her hand off. "I'm going into work. Lock the door when you leave."

I grab my keys off the counter and walk out. If I don't, I'll say something I regret. We both need time to cool off.

26

dylan

I DON'T THINK they meant for me to hear their conversation. At least, I hope they didn't. There are so many times people wish they could be a fly on the wall. To find out what people say behind closed doors. I got to experience it, and I'll just say it fucking sucks. And hurts. Every word Mrs. Donovan threw out hit each one of my nerves. Every fucking pain point I've had about the reasons why Angie wouldn't be with me.

Angie is the only person I wish I could hear. She remained calm, I think. At least her voice didn't carry through the thin walls. I hope she came to my defense, but I can't be sure. I'm still stunned she never mentioned whatever this is we're doing to her mom. All this time I thought her parents knew. I should have found it weird they hadn't invited us over for dinner. But if I'm being honest, I didn't give it much thought. Being with her overshadowed everything.

A text comes through my phone, but I don't look at it. I'm hauling ass to the lake to hang out with Jake and his family. It's going to be needed for more than catching up. I'm out of my depth here. Let's hope he actually has some advice for me.

I pull onto the road leading to the lake. There's a swimming spot that doesn't have a ton of people. We discovered it in high school and it's become our place to hang out. We don't have to worry about anyone bugging us and we won't bother other lake goers.

I see him standing next to the girl from the tattoo shop. I can't remember her name. After that fight in the field between Jake and Randall, I distanced myself from the entire group. No longer wanting to be a part of the drama. No longer feeling like I was actually included in their friendship.

I park next to his truck and get out, happy I put my swimming trunks in the car before I went to Angie's. I had hoped to talk her into coming, but I obviously didn't get the chance. At the sound of my door closing, Jake turns around and waves. You'd think he heard my car pulling up. It's not exactly quiet.

"Hey man," he pulls me in for a hug. "You remember Charleigh?"

"Vaguely," I wince. It's not a hard name to remember, and I don't know how I forgot it. "It's nice to meet you again."

"Nice to meet you, too. At least when you're sober and not coming in the shop for a tattoo." She turns to the little girl tugging on the edge of her dress and picks her up. "I'm not sure if you ever officially met this one. This is Layla, my bonus daughter."

"Leigh, I want to go swim." She gazes at the water as if it's her long-lost love. She is a spitting image of Tonya. Let's just hope she has her mama's chill demeanor.

"In just a little bit." Charleigh sets her down. "Can you say hi to Dylan?"

She eyes me up and down, skeptical about my sudden presence. I don't blame her. This kid doesn't know me. I may have been close with her parents back in high school, but I haven't been in her life. I'm a stranger. "Hi."

"How are you?" I bend down to get on her level. Maybe that will be less scary for her.

"I'm fine, but I want to go in the water." She glances behind her again, making sure the lake hasn't moved.

"I don't blame you," I grin. "Your parents and I used to hang out in this very spot when we were kids."

"You went in the water *alone*?"

"Yes,' I laugh. "We were a lot older than you. One day when you're much bigger, you'll be able to in alone too."

"I wish I was bigger now."

You think that now, kid. But the bigger you get, the more pain and confusion mess with you. "Can I steal your dad for a bit?"

"Are you going to give him back?" She crosses her arms and stares at me. She's terrifying for such a little person. Her attitude is almost a perfect mixture of Jake and Tonya. She asks questions, but isn't afraid to let you know she gets what she wants.

"Yes, sweetie," Jake scoops her up. "Dylan and I will hang out here and watch over your brother while Charleigh takes you in the water."

The woman in question rolls her eyes at the questioning look he gives her. They have their own language. I never thought I'd see Jake connect with someone like that. I was wrong. He's found someone who will do anything for him and their family. "Let's go, Layla. Grab the ball and we can toss it to each other."

Layla runs to get her ball and yells in the direction of her stepmom. "I can't forget my jumper. I don't want to get taken away to the middle."

"Smart kid you got there," I tell Jake as we watch his daughter put on her swim vest.

"I'd like to say she gets her brains from me, but we both know that's a lie. She is her mother made over with tiny hints of the influence Charleigh has had on her."

"So, what you're saying is you're basically chopped liver."

"Pretty much." He points to the sleeping baby in the stroller. "I have a feeling Asa here is going to be more like me. He's definitely vocal for such a tiny thing."

"Asa?"

"Yeah, Charleigh heard it in a show and she was dead-set on that being his name. It's not like I put up much of a fight. I'd let her do anything she wanted."

"It must be nice." I sit down in one of the collapsible chairs by the stroller.

"Things rocking with you and Ang?" He sits down next to me, making sure both the baby and the rest of his family are in view. He really has grown up. He's a completely different person than I remember and I wish I had reached out to him. and the rest of our friends, after my football accident.

"You could say that." I squirm. I'm not used to talking about my feelings with him, but he's the person I have right now, and I could really use his advice.

"What happened?" He reaches in the cooler and grabs two beers, handing me one of them.

I tell him about what I overhead at her house before deciding to come here early. How her mom went from being the same sweet woman I remembered her to be, to judgmental at the mention of Angie and I dating. It was like getting whiplash.

"I overhead parts of the conversation. Mostly her mom yelling about how much younger I am than her. How it couldn't work. And why didn't Angie tell them about us dating? If she was ashamed to let them know."

"Wow. That's...a lot."

"You're telling me."

"What did Angie say?"

"I couldn't hear her for the most part. The only part I did hear is her saying she asked her brother to keep our relationship secret from their parents. I don't know even know what to do with that information."

"Have you talked to her?"

"No. I left her a text saying I was coming here early. And, my phone dinged when I was on my way here but I didn't check to see who it was. I was hoping she'd come here after her mom left. It doesn't look like that's happening, though."

"Maybe she'll show up later."

"Doubt it. If I had to guess, I'm betting she went to work. It's what she does when she wants to lose herself in something."

"Is this where *you* need to be? I wouldn't hold it against you if you left to check in with Angie."

"I know. But I need this space to think. I kind of figured this may end up happening when I pursued her. She was reluctant to give us a shot, and I pushed until she finally said okay."

Jake laughs, and Asa stirs in his stroller. "I saw the way she looked at you when you met us there. She wanted you just as much as you wanted her. Just give her time."

"Well, that time is running out."

"Why is that? Is there something you're not telling me? Like something serious?"

"Nothing like that. Mom is getting better. More mobile with every day that passes. As soon as she can drive herself without me worrying, I need to head back home."

"Oh." There's sadness there. For the time we missed growing into our new lives together I'm guessing. It amazes me we were able to pick up where we left off, like we hadn't burned bridges after that first summer home. "Probably should have seen that coming. I was kind of hoping you'd stick around Asheville. Then we could really get the whole group back together."

"It's not a done deal. Not yet, anyway. There's a good chance I may come back."

"Really?"

"Yeah. The shop I've been working at cut some staff, and I drew one of the lucky numbers. I have applications in at other shops, and I'm waiting to hear back. Plus, I'm sure my apartment is dusty as hell."

"Is that where you really want to be, though?"

I shrug. "Not sure yet. It depends if there's anything here worth staying for."

"Geez, maybe I really am chopped liver. Even if things don't work out with you and Angie, we are here. *Your friends.* You know the people you grew up with."

"I know that. And if I go back and stay, I won't go so long without visits. I realized lately how much I've truly missed y'all. Things weren't always sunshine and rainbows when we were teens, but I let that hurt dictate my life for way too long. I should have been here with you guys, getting to know your families."

"Damn straight." Just then Layla rushes up the sanded area and plops herself in Jake's lap. She's soaking wet, and I'm happy as hell I don't have kids. I need to figure my life out before I even go down that road.

"You two have a nice chat?" Charleigh is making her way toward us.

"I think so?" Jake says it more like a question than a statement.

"That sounds promising." She grabs one of the towels on the blanket they've laid out and wraps it around her. "I'm going to grill these hot dogs. It's your turn to take Layla out there. She wants to go deeper than I'm comfortable taking her."

"Fine, fine." Jake stands, tossing Layla a few inches in the air and catching her. Her joyous laughter filling our area. "Let's go to the deep. But you better save me if a big fish tries to bite my toe."

"You're so silly, Daddy." I watch my friend go to the waters edge with is daughter in his arms before rushing in, splashing everywhere.

"I'll be right back. I'm going to see if my mom needs anything when I head back."

"Go on," I've got this.

I head to my car and grab my phone. When I unlock my phone, I see the text, but it's not from a number I recognize.

UNKNOWN

> Hi Dylan, I sent you an email, but I'm not sure you got it. If you're still interested in working at our shop, I'd like to set up an interview.

I almost drop my phone. That is unexpected. I open up my mail app, and scroll through the unread messages until I find the one asking for an interview. This could change everything.

27

angie

THE BAR ISN'T AS busy as it has been, which is odd for a weekend. It's gorgeous outside, though. I imagine a lot of folks are soaking up the sun. Not that I blame them. I could have been until Mom came by and screwed it up. I heard her call after me when I stormed out of my house, but I didn't have anything to say. And, honestly, she doesn't deserve an explanation. Should I have mentioned dating Dylan to them? Probably. But that didn't give her the right to come question me. Especially after he showed up. I mean, who does that?

Lisa comes through the front doors and stops when she sees me. "Are you supposed to be off today?"

Before I can form a response, Carlos butts in. "Yes. And I'd appreciate if she went back home."

"What?" I whirl on him. "It's my bar. How in the hell are you going to tell me to leave?"

He waves his hand in my direction and raises an

eyebrow. "Because you are in a mood and the customers can tell. They whisper when you walk away with their orders."

"Let them," I huff.

"Did something happen?" Lisa approaches me slowly. Like I'm a wild animal that will spook if she gets too close.

Do I say anything? They are both already so engrained in my life. I don't know that I should drag them into my love life, especially after I told Carlos it was off limits.

"I don't really want to talk about it."

"Because that's healthy." Carlos doesn't bat an eye when I glare at him.

"It's just things with Dylan, and then my mom." I sigh and rub my forehead, trying to force away the headache I can feel coming on.

Things were so much simpler when the only thing I focused on was the bar. Then in walks Dylan and I lose my shit in a matter of weeks. My life feels like a rom-com gone wrong right now and I don't know how to deal with it.

"That sounds like a possible bad situation." Lisa rubs my back. I want to lean into her, but I feel like a moron needing support from someone so much younger than me.

And that's the root of the problem. Dylan is the same age as Lisa. I've always looked at her as being one of my close friends, but with him it's different. I've heard the whispers from customers, but I shoved them aside. My business is none of theirs. Except they may have a point. We are from two different worlds. But for him, that doesn't seem to matter. Why am I so caught up with what people think of me? I never have been before.

"You don't know the half of it." Frustration runs through every nerve of my body. I should have gone to the lake and talked to him. It's been hours and I don't have any idea where his head is at. If he even wants to continue this tryst we have after hearing my mom lose her shit. Now, it may be too late.

Lisa glances at Carlos, then back at me. As if I can't see them having a silent conversation about what to do with me. "Look, I know you want to forget your problems for a bit, but being here isn't going to make that happen. Why don't you go home and chill out for a bit? Or, go look for Dylan. I'm sure he'd like to hear what was said."

"I highly doubt that," I laugh. It's bitter and ragged. "I know for a fact he heard every word she said. Mom wasn't exactly quiet in her protestations."

"Then go to him and figure it out. You each deserve that. To see where both of you stand."

She's right. It's what I should do. I'm terrified, though. What if he takes what my mom said to heart? The age thing does trip me up sometimes, but I can work past that...I think.

"Seriously, Angie," Carlos's voice is low enough to not be heard by everyone else, but it's urgent. "If you do not get out of this bar and figure life out, I'm going to quit."

"No, you won't." He can't. I'd be lost without him and Lisa.

"If you say so," he rolls his eyes. "Just go talk to him. I can't deal with you being all mopey and sad."

"Fine," I huff. When did my employees get so bossy? Let's be real, they are more than that. They've been there for me more than others. I don't know what I'd do without them. The only people that would make this circle complete are Stella and Johnny. "I'll go see if he's home. He went to the lake with Jake today, and I'm not sure if he's back yet."

"Then you wait at his house until he does get home."

Lisa says while pushing me toward the door. Carlos follows behind us with my bag in his hand.

"Where did you even get that? It was in the office." He shoves it in my hand before going back to the bar to do his job.

"I grabbed it while you were waiting tables. I was only waiting for the right time to kick you out of here."

"Wow. Thanks for that, I guess. It doesn't feel so great being on the receiving end of getting forced out, by the way."

"It's not supposed to," Lisa giggles. "Now, go make smart decisions before I call in sick and take you there myself."

"Angie get out of here because Lisa is not going anywhere. I need her today."

"Maybe I should st—" I begin but Carlos cuts me off.

"If you don't get out that door."

I don't give him a chance to finish the statement and haul ass out the door. It may have taken some convincing, but they are right. I need to go see Dylan.

* * *

Dylan's car isn't home when I pull up to the curb. The sun is setting, so he should be home soon. I can either be a creeper and stay in the car, or knock on the door. Surely his mom will let me in. Unlike my terrified ass, she knows all about us. All of this could have been avoided if I had put on my big girl panties and talked to my parents.

I get out of the car and shut the door behind me. My steps are slow and shaky as I make my way to the door. I feel like a scared child. Not knowing what could happen when he gets home. My hand raps on the door three times and I wait.

I hear the cane she's started using recently. It's been a nice upgrade from the walker. I know how much she hated that thing, After a few minutes, the door opens and the smile she's wearing is so big. I hope like hell she can't see the fear that has to be written across mine.

"I didn't expect to see you tonight," she pulls me in for a hug. "Dylan said you had some last-minute things to do with your mom."

Good. At least he didn't tell her that my mom acted like a heinous person while he was in the next room. "Yeah, it was out of the blue."

"Well, he's not back yet, but you can come in and wait. I'm just watching a movie and eating some popcorn. I can make more if you want some."

"Oh, no, I'm fine. But I'll wait inside with you." She moves back and I follow her inside. In the short amount of time I've been dating Dylan, this house has almost become a second home. Not because I don't like hanging out with my parents, but because I like seeing his mom have some down-time. Despite the broken foot, this is probably the first time I've seen her slow down and take care of herself. She more than deserves it.

A chick flick is playing on the screen. She curls up on the couch with her foot propped up and pulls a blanket over her. I sit in the recliner on the other side of the room. Does hiding in the shadows make me a creeper? Possibly. But it'll give me a chance to prepare whatever I'm going to say when Dylan walks through that door. I'll also be able to study him for a second before he notices me. Judge the mood he's in.

The movie is almost over when the front door opens.

His mom has dozed off on the couch. I feel awful for not being able to take her for lunch today. I'll have to make it up to her later. Waiting for him to come into the living room is torture, and I wonder if sitting over here was a bad idea.

Finally, the door closes and his footsteps approach. He doesn't miss a beat when he enters the living room. He makes note of his mom sleeping on the couch and makes his way toward me. He doesn't seem angry. That's a plus, but I won't really know until he says something. I have always been able to tell his mood based on how strained his words are.

"How long have you been here?"

"Since the movie started. Your mom fell asleep about halfway through. How did you know I was here?"

"Your car is parked right outside the house. I figured that was a good indication."

Duh, Angie. Of course, he was going to see the car. "Oh yeah." He starts to sit on the floor next to me, but I stop him. "Actually, can we go in the backyard and talk?"

"Is this about earlier?" His voice is tight. While he may not be mad, he's definitely hurt by the words my mom spewed.

"Yeah. I feel like I need to explain myself."

"Okay." He holds his hand out, waiting for me to take it. "There's something I want to talk to you about, too."

A ball of dread forms in the pit of my stomach. Reluctantly, I take his hand and let him pull me up. He leads me through the living room, into the kitchen, and out the back door of the house. There's a small bench under a tree at the far end, and I follow him to it.

Once we sit down, I pull my hands into my lap, wringing them. Here goes nothing. We'll either be okay, or we won't.

28

dylan

SHE SEEMS NERVOUS. Is it good or bad? I guess I won't know until she actually says something. "Before you start, I have to know one thing. Are you ashamed of dating me because of the age thing?"

She snaps her head back. "Of course, not. It's something I've been constantly working through, but I'm not ashamed."

"What is there to work through?"

"Sometimes it seems like we're from two separate worlds. There are things you like that I have no interest in. And a part of me wonders if the differences will be a deal breaker in the future."

"That's your problem, though. You spend so much time thinking about the future that you don't live in the here and now."

"Which is one of the things I'm working on." She ticks an errant stand of hair behind her ear. "I do want to see where this goes. It's scary. As shocking as it is, despite my age, I've never been in a serious relationship. All of that has always come second to the bar, and not everyone appreciates me choosing an inanimate thing over them."

And we're back to her original argument. Now is my chance to drop my news on her and see how she responds. I need to know now more than ever. "I got a request for a job interview."

"Oh."

"Seriously, that's it. Just 'oh'. I'm asking you if you want me to take it, or if you and I are going to be a real thing. If you're willing to ignore gossip or other people's opinions and give us an actual shot."

She doesn't say anything. Eyes wide in shock and mouth wide open.

"Dammit, Angie. I love you. I think I have since I understood what love really meant. I need to know if what we have is worth fighting for."

She stands and looks down on me. "Of course, it is. How could you even think it wouldn't be?"

Finally, the fire and passion I saw in her the first day we were together. She's taking control of the situation, but I still need to know that I'm it for her. That I'm what she truly wants. That aside from my mom and friends, I have a home here. Someone to come home to at the end of the day. Because if she's not all in, I don't know that I can stay and act like everything is okay. I might be selfish for wanting that, but I don't care. Love is the one thing I want to be selfish about.

"Because you didn't shut down whatever you mom was saying. Or, maybe the fact that you never told your parents we were seeing each other."

"It's not because I was ashamed."

"Then why?" She won't say if I don't push her. Hell, I

had to push her to admit she felt something toward me. We haven't been together long, but I know who I want. And where I want to be.

She throws her hands up in the air. "I don't know any other way to prove it to you. I didn't want to tell them because I didn't know if we were going to last. What's the point in introducing the person you're with to your parents if you have no idea what the future holds? That's why I didn't tell them. Not because of our age difference, not because I'm ashamed. If anything, other than the bar, you are my bright spot in the day. You make me feel like I can have more than just the bar. That I can have an actual life. And that I'm capable of being happy outside of it."

Well, that's not what I was expecting. But it does make me feel better. She does care. It might not be love for her yet. But at least she knows how deeply I feel for her. I still need to know what she wants me to do about the job.

"So, do you want me to go on the interview? Because honestly, you are the only thing keeping me here. The only reason I would want to stay. I need to know that you're done running."

"No," she stammers.

"No, what? I'm going to need a little more than that." There are a lot of things she could be responding to, and I need clear-cut, definitive answers.

"No, I don't want you to go on the stupid interview. I want you here, where you belong, in your hometown. Working at my bar, or hell even working at Johnny's shop. I just know I don't want you far away from me. I know people make long-distance relationships work, but if I'm in I'm all in. And I can't be all in with you if you're in another state."

That's it. Those are the words I needed to hear. I needed

to know. That she wants me here. That being with me is worth the risk for her. It's one of my insecurities, and I know it is. Everyone else in my life didn't want me around. Dad bailed when I was a baby. My friends treated me like I was an accessory, and my team ditched me when I was injured. If she didn't want me as well, I wouldn't be able to take it. She said it, though. She's all in with me. If that means staying in the town I ran away from, I'll do it. This place deserves a second chance. Especially now, seeing it through adult eyes.

I pull her into my lap, curling my fingers in her hair before crashing my lips into hers. Letting her know exactly how I feel without words. Now I feel complete. I feel like I'm home for the first time in my life.

There was a slim chance I would have stayed without her by my side. But it would have been hard. There's no way in hell I would have been able to go into the bar again, much less work there. But knowing she's here with me. Knowing that she is all in, it's enough...for now. I know she loves me in her own way, and I'll wait until she's ready to say the words.

Her hands grip my shirt and I start to pull it off, giving her access to all of me. She stops kissing me and laughs. "Dylan, we're outside. There's no way in hell we're having sex in your backyard when your mom is in the living room and anyone in the neighborhood could see us."

"I thought you weren't worried about what other people thought."

"About us being together? Not in the slightest." She kisses my cheek. "But I don't want anyone else seeing my goods, or yours."

"You have a point. I am the only one who gets to see you naked from now on."

"Same goes for you buddy," she bops me on the nose, and swat her hand away. "How about we go back inside? I'm sure you'll want to tell your mom you're staying in town."

"Yeah, then I guess it's all logistics from there." Finding an apartment is the first thing on my list. I love my mom and being here to help out when she needs it, but there's no way in hell I'm screwing the girl of my dreams in my childhood bed with her across the hall.

"We'll figure it out." She climbs out of my lap and holds her hand out to pull me up. "One thing at a time."

It's nice hearing her say that instead of focusing on all the what-ifs. Her phone dings in her pocket and she pulls it out. "Is everything okay?"

Opening the screen, she sighs. "Not really. Any chance you want to go break up a fight?"

"Carlos, or the other staff, can't handle it?"

She shows me the screen.

CARLOS

I think there's about to be a fight between two customers. Calling the cops, but if you can get lover boy over here to handle it, that would probably be easier.

"Did he have to refer to me as that?"

"I guess so. I went to the bar after you left instead of going after you. He practically kicked me out. He must have had more faith we'd work it out than I did."

"Honestly, there wasn't much to work out. I only needed to know where you stood."

"I'll stand anywhere as long as you're by my side. I think we make a pretty good team."

"Yep," I nod. We walk toward the side gate, bypassing the inside of the house completely. I'll text my mom and let her know where I am. There's no time to change. "Aren't you glad you decided to keep me around? Who would take care of the dumbasses if I left?"

She looks me over as we head around the house. "No idea, but I'll put my money on you, swim trunks and all, any day of the week."

I pull her close to me as we approach her car. "It'll be more embarrassing for the guys getting tossed out than for me." She unlocks the car and once we're both inside, I turn toward her. "We probably need to look into hiring a full-time bouncer. Especially with the live music opening soon. Can you imagine getting interrupted in the middle of sex?"

"Oh my god," she groans. "You can't talk about hiring someone and sex in the same conversation. I only focus on the latter."

"Good," I grin. She starts the car and puts it in drive. I reach over, putting my hand on her thigh. All those times I imagined doing just this when I was a teen paid off in the end. My childhood crush lasted through the years, and she's finally mine.

epilogue

THE ENTIRE STAFF is sitting around three tables pushed together. It's normal for a Sunday morning. We have them every week. But this time, we have more employees. There's even an actual bouncer filling one of the seats. We've hired more people in the months since the job fair. Apparently, all we had to do was send out a mass help wanted signal, and people showed up ready to do the job.

The only person missing is Lisa. She wanted to explore the world, and we all wished her well. She has been and will always be an integral part of the team. If she ever decides to come back, I'll welcome her with open arms. The only thing I'm sad about is not being able to send her to bartending school. She would have made a killing, pouring drinks for our customers.

Stella is standing at the end, asking us all for our attention. "As you know the renovation on the other space is almost done. That means we're going to have to do some training for how the space will work once it's open. I'm going to bring in some people from a few of the bars my cousin frequents in Austin."

Dylan is sitting beside me, his finger tracing circles on my leg. Stella is still talking, and I've all but tuned her out. I keep pushing him to go see Johnny about a job, doing something he loves, but he always tells me he will when he's ready. The past few months with him have been amazing. I can't believe I fought him so hard on being in a relationship. The fact I don't have to choose between him and the bar is even better. He supports me one hundred percent. He's never made me feel like I'm unevenly splitting my time between them, and I love him for that.

I still haven't said the words out loud. I think he knows, but I need to tell him. Soon, maybe even today.

He squeezes my leg and nods toward Stella. "She's calling your name."

"Oops, sorry." I don't even know what she was saying, since I've been trapped in my own head. Grateful for all I've accomplished. "Thanks for the update, Stella. Any questions about how things will work in the future should be sent to her. Carlos will also be available for any help the new bartenders need." I see two of the women we hired shoot him appreciative glances. I'm almost certain he's the reason they applied. "That pretty much sums up the meeting. There are donuts on the table, so you can help yourself. Those of you on the schedule today, I'll see you in a few hours."

Everyone gets up and does their own thing. Carlos goes to the bar and makes sure it's stocked for the rest of the day. The door opens and closes so much in the next few minutes I don't notice Reaf's sister standing inside. "Are y'all open?"

She's been coming here a lot lately. Usually once a week, but not with a little boy standing beside her. I knew she had a kid, but I forgot how much he's grown since the last time I saw him.

"No, no—," Carlos clears his throat. His eyes are focused solely on her. "Not yet. We open in a couple of hours."

"Crap. I'm so sorry," she turns back toward the door. Carlos watches her the entire way.

Once she's outside, I smirk. "So, do you have something you want to tell us?"

Dylan leans on the counter watching the interaction. He doesn't work today, but likes to help get everything set up with us. "I think someone has a crush."

Carlos groans. "And I think someone needs to keep their damn mouth shut."

"That's not very nice." I've noticed since she started coming, he's the only one who will wait on her. One time one of the guys tried, and he directed him to the other side of the bar. He doesn't know who she is since he's not from around here. He didn't grow up with everyone else. Hell, I'm shocked she's been going out.

"Shut up," he rolls his eyes. "And I need more napkins from storage."

"I've got them," Dylan says. Still doing everything he can to avoid Carlos when he's in a mood. He rushes to the office to take care of it.

"Don't hound me, Ang. This is one of those things that's off-limits."

"Fine," I put my hands up in surrender because I don't want him to feel like I'm prying. "I'll go help Dylan with the napkins."

I keep my steps soft as I make my way to the office. He has his hands in the air, a box in one hand, and he's trying to pull another one down with the other. "You look like you could use a hand."

He startles and drops the box in his hand, turning toward me. "Dammit, Angie."

"Sucks, doesn't it?" Before he can move, I jump into his arms, clinging to him like a tree. There's a plus side to being shorter than him.

"What are you doing?" He glances behind him, but I turn his head toward me. "Carlos could come back here at any moment."

He's not wrong. Carlos is the one who interrupted us all those months ago. We've come full circle. "Possibly, but," I give him a quick peck. "I couldn't care less. I love you and what he thinks doesn't really matter."

He sucks in a breath at my admission. "Those are the three words I've been waiting ages for you to say. I love you, too. And if we were the only ones here, I would shove everything off the desk and fuck you senseless."

"I can always tell Carlos to go home."

"No, I'm still trying to get in his good graces. But one day...you, me, and that desk have a date."

"Deal." He sets me down and I help him pick up the extra aprons that fell out of the box. We're running out and I'll need to order more if we hire anyone else. I hope Uncle Max is proud of me. I feel like I've turned this place into a community staple, even on the hard nights. And I've found someone to spend my time with who makes me happier than I've ever been. With my friends and Dylan surrounding me, I know we can do so much more for what was once a hole in the wall bar.

***

Geez, I need to remember I'm not as young as I used to be. Not that I went out much then. I was too busy trying to build a life with Nathan. That obviously didn't work out.

Out of the Ashes is modern and old at the same time. I remember when Angie's uncle owned the place before he passed away. I was still a teenager, but everyone knew this place.

It's right on the edge of downtown Asheville. I can't count how many times some group of nay-sayers tried to get it shut down. In their opinion, the clientele wasn't savory, and they didn't want that sort of trouble so close to the boutiques. It never when through. Thank goodness. If it had we'd have nowhere close by to hang out. We'd have to drive an hour to Dallas, or go to one of the neighboring towns. Since high school rivalries are a thing, none of us do that too often.

"Hey," Sam nudges my shoulder. "I'm going to grab us another drink. What do you want?"

"Surprise me." I grin. It's one of the few nights I can kick back and relax with my friends. I love David with all my heart. He's my reason for living, but sometimes a mom needs a little me time.

"You shouldn't have told her that," Kate laughs. "She's going to come back with something that will knock you on your ass."

I shrug. If she does, I'll call my mom or Reaf to come pick me up. Hell, I'll ask Bryce if I have to. Actually, that's a good idea. I've already had a couple of drinks and there's no way I'm getting behind the wheel.

Pulling out my phone, I shoot off a text to my baby brother. He's honestly the best option. Assuming he isn't somewhere hanging out with his friends. It's been a whole semester since he's seen them and I remember how that felt all too well.

BRYCE

You got it.

CAROLINE

You don't have plans?

BRYCE

Not until this weekend. Everyone is
being respectable and looking for
summer jobs.

CAROLINE

Okay. Thank you broski.

BRYCE

Have a fun kid free night.

BRYCE

And don't ever call me that again. Lame.

Laughing I put my phone back in my pocket. He may act like he hates the nickname, but I think he secretly loves it. Once Reaf and Tonya got married, he and I became closer than I ever thought. I'm honestly not sure how I would have handled being home with only mom all the time. I mean, she's been amazing since the divorce, but nothing says spinster like hanging out with your mom on Friday nights.

"Please tell me whoever you're texting isn't related to you." Emily comes around the high top table and gives me a hug.

"I was arranging for my brother to pick me up when we're done here. Thank you very much." I push her away. "It's about time you showed up."

"Sorry," she grimaces. "My mom called and you know

how she can be. Always meddling and trying to set me up with one of her friends' son. It's annoying."

I shudder at the thought. My mom tried that once and after my reaction, never did it again. I don't want anything long term. Or well, even short term. Taking care of a kid and working full time has me busy enough. Nights like this are my one indulgence.

"So, any cute guys from out of town come in?" Emily sets her wallet on the table and waves at Sam. "Please tell me she went up there for a refill. I need a drink after all that nonsense."

"Yep," Kate laughs. "You can have mine since I'm sure she already ordered our drinks. I'll go grab my own. You need to catch up."

"It's not like we didn't see each other earlier today." I shake my head. "I mean we do work together."

"True," Emily taps the table. "The only difference is, that was work time. This is our playtime."

"You make it sound so dirty." Kate takes the final drink from her glass before heading to the bar to help Sam and get another drink.

"So, are you going to find some trouble tonight?"

I hate the fact this question gets brought up every week. We all went to school together. We lost touch after Nathan and I got married. Even back then, when he and I were high school sweethearts, they never liked him.

Once they found out we were heading for divorce and I needed a job, they didn't hesitate to hire me on at the floral business they had recently started together. It took a while to take off, but with small town weddings becoming popular, we occasionally have to turn people away now.

"Are we really going to do this again?"

"You never know. You could find "Mister Right" in this very bar. But you'll never know because you don't put yourself out there."

"Honestly, who in their right mind would want to date a woman that comes with baggage."

"Your brother did."

"He's an exception to the rule. Reaf has always been wiser beyond his years."

Sam and Kate are back at the table, efficiently putting an end to the conversation. "What did we miss?" Sam sets a drink in front of me and another one in front of Emily.

"Oh, nothing." Emily takes a sip of her drink before making a face. "Why does this taste like tequila?"

"Oh shit," Sam covers her mouth. "That was for Caroline."

"Oh no. I did not ask for tequila."

"You told me to surprise you." She holds her hands in the air and wiggles her fingers. "Surprise!"

"How about I go grab another beer, and you take this one?"

"You're no fun," Sam pouts.

"Yes I am," I laugh as I turn from the table. "I just don't need tequila to make me that way."

The three of them are giggling as I walk away from the table. I can only imagine what they're talking about as soon as I'm out of earshot. Probably figuring out who they are going to set me up with. And Emily talks about her mom meddling. Those three are just as bad. If not worse.

Even though it's a Wednesday, Out of the Ashes is busier than normal. I weave through groups dancing to the music coming through the speaker. The space they have next door needs to hurry up and be done. Then these people can go over there and those of us who only want to hang out can occupy this space. I don't have anything against dancing, but I've been almost knocked over too many times to count.

Finding an empty space at the bar is close to impossible, but the second one opens up, I squeeze in. I'm not loud enough to be heard over multiple people.

A guy, younger than me, leans over to take my order. I open my mouth but he's redirected before I can even place my order. Now, Carlos, the head bartender, is standing in front of me. A tall glass of beer in front of him.

"Is that for me?" I can't help the blush I'm sure is present.

"Yes." Short and to the point. "I got it ready as soon as I noticed you coming this way. I tried talking your friend out of the drink she got you, but she didn't listen."

"Thank you." I reach for the glass and our fingers meet for the briefest moment. He's attractive, and if I didn't have a little person that depended on me, I'd probably ask him on a date. But I do, and there's no point.

When I turn back toward the table, I notice all three of my friends staring in my direction. The second they see me looking back, they turn around. Why do I feel like I was just set up?

Sam has a shit-eating grin when I get back to my side of the table. "You ordered that drink on purpose, didn't you?"

"Maybe."

I point a finger at Kate. "Did you know?"

She shrugs and doesn't say a word. She totally knew. I don't know why they are so fixated on me finding someone. I've told them time and time again that I have zero interest.

"Don't be mad," Kate finally says. "But we know you think he's hot, even if he is a little older."

"And," Sam butts in. "From the way he's always looking at you, he feels the same."

"It doesn't matter," I throw my hands in the air, inches from hitting a waitress walking behind me. "I don't want any sort of relationship. I've got David to think about. And right now, it hits a little harder than normal."

"Oh shit," Emily gasps. "I completely forgot it's almost the anniversary of that time."

Yeah, that's putting it mildly. It's been almost six years since Nathan and I have split up. I don't still harbor feelings for him, but he's already been remarried and divorced since then. He could move on so quickly. And to this day I can't find it in me to trust anyone else.

"Yeah." The good time I was having is brought down by the mention of my ex. You'd think I'd be over it by now, but the sting of rejection is something I still feel. It's one of the reasons I don't date. The other reason is hopefully asleep with my mom watching over him.

"Sorry," Emily whispers. "I didn't mean to bring it front and center." The music is loud and the people yelling to be heard at the tables next to us make it hard to hear what she's said, but I get the gist.

"It's all good." I plaster a fake smile across my face. My friends see right through it. They keep their mouths closed, though. Willing to fake it right along with me. "Let's not mention horrible exes for the rest of the night. I still have a bit before my baby brother will be here to pick me up, and we're here to have a good time."

"Speaking of baby brothers," Kate waggles her eyebrows up and down. "Is he single?"

I choke on the drink I just took and almost spit beer everywhere. "You are not dating my baby brother." I wipe my mouth in case any liquid managed to escape. "Remember, we had a rule, no siblings."

"Yeah, yeah," Kate waves my words away. "I know. No siblings. In my defense, you shouldn't have good looking brothers."

"Gross." I groan. "Okay, let's move on from that subject."

I know she's only doing it to get under my skin, but it still grosses me out. They are my brothers. She's never had to worry about that aspect with her friends liking her siblings. She's an only child. The rest of us know the feeling all too well.

"Okay," Sam snorts. "Can we talk about the wedding for the bridezilla we have coming up?"

"I'm guessing she made more changes?" I sigh.

"Yep," Emily crosses her arms on the table. "She called right after you left asking us if we could change the flower type."

"You told her no, right?"

Kate is already shaking her head. "Nope. We did say that this was the last change."

"That's good, at least." We've got to get the contract updated to say no changes so many days before a wedding.

"We may need to cancel next week's hangout, though." Emily groans.

That's going to suck, but I get it. Their, no our, first priority is the client. The shop is finally getting some buzz, and we need to do whatever we can to keep that coming. Now if I could remember I'm an actual part of the team, and not someone they pity.

Sam taps the table with her knuckles. "One last round before we head home?"

"Yes," we all say in unison.

"But nothing heavy for me. I still have to get David ready for school," I add.

Sam mutters something about weekends when she leaves the table. They'll understand when they have kids. Aside from the flower shop, David is my biggest priority. And he always will be.

acknowledgments

This has been the book of my heart for years. I've been thinking about it for so long. It was supposed to be the book I dove into after finishing Gone Again. Two years of burnout halted it until I came out of it.

I want to say a huge thank you to all the readers. Thank you for waiting for me to return to writing. Thank you for supporting me through the hard times.

My Alpha team...y'all are the best. This book probably wouldn't be done if it wasn't for your encouragement. And I promise I'll never ask about fade to black scenes again. :P

Thank you to my team, y'all keep me organized, and I couldn't do any of this without you!

My family and friends, thank you for always having my back. For listening to me complain about how hard writing is some days. For giving me the time I needed to finish this. Just your constant support. Thank you and I love you.

also by katrina marie

Out of the Ashes

Cocktails & Crushes

Brews & Bartenders

Mai Tais & Mistletoe

Martinis & Musicians

The Taking Chances Series

Welcome to Your Life

Cruel and Beautiful World

Ways to Go

Remember That Night

My Only Wish is You

From This Moment

Shoot Down the Stars

Love Will Save Your Soul

Take a Chance

Cousins Gone RomCom Series

Gone Country

Gone Steady

Gone Again

Cocky Hero Club

Big Baller

Silverwood Bulldog Series

Baseball & Broadway

about the author

Katrina Marie lives in the Dallas area with her husband, two children, and fur baby. She is a lover of all things geeky and nerdy. When she's not writing you can find her at her children's sporting events, or curled up reading a book.

You can find Katrina Marie online in the following places:

Sign up for my newsletter: https://www.subscribepage.com/KatrinaMarieNewsletter

Website: katrinamarieauthor.com

facebook.com/katrinamarieauthor

twitter.com/katmarieauthor

instagram.com/katrinamarieauthor

bookbub.com/profile/katrina-marie

pinterest.com/katrinamarieauthor

tiktok.com/@katrinamarieauthor

patreon.com/katrinamarie